From Now Until the End of Time
Men of Neptune 5

By

Deja Black

Dedication

For every writer who dreams.
Keep writing.

Chapter One

It was not enough that Gavin's friend Pauric continued to pepper him with what he considered well-thought-out reasons, but he also swam around Orin, attempting to distract him while he tended his coral garden.

Nothing gave Orin more pleasure than working the reefs, distributing the vital minerals needed to improve their glory. Tending the purples and reds, the brilliant yellows and blues of the living corals, and the creatures that made their home among the nooks and crannies, like the sea anemone waving their tentacles invitingly. If anyone wanted to find him, they need only visit the reef, where he spent his time relaxing and finding his calm. When he wasn't fighting, training, or listening to his people's concerns, he sought peace in his garden.

And, of course, Pauric knew this. His role in Orin's world was more of a brother than a friend, no matter what silliness he currently displayed.

"What do you want, clownfish?" Orin remarked.

Pauric was without his ebony trident with its sparkling tips, a striking complement to his reddish hair. Yet the merman still resembled a clownfish, his antics supporting the perception.

"It's nesting season." Pauric smirked as he swam backward, a brow lifted and his arms crossed.

It wasn't as if Orin didn't know that nesting season marked the time merpeople would try their hardest to find their mate. Most merfolk were convinced that a random series of dates in Neptune's calendar would suddenly make such an impossible task probable for all.

Ridiculous.

Orin didn't believe it and refused to entertain his tragically romantic friend. He admired Pauric's hopes, but setting such a goal for himself merely frustrated him. He had better things to do with his time.

Nudging the manta ray sliding along his side out of his way, he dipped a hand inside his bucket. He gathered a handful of plankton, groaning when the manta moved in and bumped him again, the flirt. Laughing, he pushed it away once more and opened his hand, allowing the plankton to fall on the reef's surface.

Pauric spun in place, his reddish curls catching the light from the sun, his scales nearly glowing. "While I admire your unfailing dedication to caring for our coral reefs, can't they sort of do that themselves?"

Orin lamented the fact that Pauric had apparently failed to listen to him in the past, clearly unable to recall the many times they'd discussed his garden. Then again, Pauric's perfectionism regarding his profession as the armorer for the Guardians of Neptune didn't necessarily lend itself to maintaining observations and random facts for other interests. Despite Pauric's forgetfulness, his constant support plus his joy and laughter had found its partner in Orin's soul.

While Pauric might not remember why Orin cared about the reef, he never forgot that he did. Hence, the buckets of plankton Pauric had procured that morning and brought to Orin for the task. He could forgive characteristics in Pauric that would typically annoy him to no end as a Tetra—leader of the Guardians—and still feel infinitely fond of his friend.

He smiled at Pauric and explained one again. "Over time and with humankind's inability to leave the natural world alone, our coral reefs suffer. They taint them, destroying them without care. As people of the sea, it is our duty to protect them. Of course, some humans work to protect this gift, but there are not enough."

Even now, as Orin sought to educate Pauric, Pauric's focus

drifted elsewhere. The familiar daze appeared whenever Orin waxed on about preserving coral reefs.

"Yes, so important." Pauric worked hard to contain a threatening yawn, but one tiny bubble escaped his lips.

Orin shook his head and went back to tending the reef.

Pauric clapped his hands. "Now, about my request. Look at that overflowing vessel there. I even found your favorite crustaceans for our friends to savor. Surely that will ease your stance and save me from another lecture." He smiled, pointing at another bucket, and the bits he'd procured were indeed lovely.

There had once been a moment when Orin believed Pauric, with his eagerness to please, could be a viable candidate for his bed. Perhaps something even more permanent. Pauric was beautiful in form and heart, supple in his movements. He would be a work of art tied up, one worthy of his brother Trillian's paintings.

But no . . .

Pauric would never submit to Orin, see Orin as the master of his body, a must Orin desired of his lovers. Simply put, he and Pauric were better as friends and brothers. Though Orin had three brothers of his blood—Kamau, Batair, and Trillian—he considered Pauric the bother of his heart.

Orin sighed. In all his years, he'd never found a lover capable of satisfying his needs adequately. He'd accepted this, making his peace with sampling nubile lovers who failed to last beyond a lustful evening. While they enjoyed each other, the need to possess never rose—the desire to mate and share young was never a consideration. Instead, he would satisfy their needs but never his own.

Orin needed to own. Mark. Destroy. Wreck. He craved his fingerprints upon flesh. He hungered to hear raw screams as he took and bruised. He visualized streaks of tears when he obtained his partner's complete submission. And then he

3

wanted to hold, gently pamper, and worship. But no one could take that. Before he could satisfy his urge to care after his joy of brutally pounding between hot thighs, words complaining of too big, too hard, too rough, and too deep would commence.

He used to believe he would find someone destined for him, but as years passed and none appeared, he surrendered that dream. He accepted.

So why, in this time of nesting, should he think differently? Did Pauric genuinely believe he should cast his hopes on a world of humans?

"I can see that logistical brain of yours questioning my sanity." Pauric broke through Orin's musing. "Why can't we at least visit the surface world and have a look? I've never been, and going without you is hardly likely unless I sneak off as some have. But I have a healthy fear of your grandfather and would like to do things with his permission. If you make the request to go, our king would be more likely to say yes."

The pleading tone in Pauric's voice was slowly breaking him down. Orin needed to remain strong and push back.

"And you've decided this how?" Orin spread another handful of plankton out before focusing on his delusional friend. "You know Neptune is not keen on sending anyone to the surface world. He commands the older mer to watch out for things like when the young venture off."

Pauric raised a finger. "Yes, but if you were to say you wished to check on your siblings and spend some time there, the desire to spy on his progeny would be difficult to resist. And, of course, one such as myself would be allowed to accompany you without question, as I am your friend."

Ah. Pauric had given this request some dedicated consideration, and he wasn't wrong in his thinking. Orin's grandfather often sought word of his grandsons and their families. So a first-hand view would go a long way to achieving a yes to traveling above.

"And you would accompany me because . . ." Orin had to know how Pauric would wrap himself into this adventure.

"Well, as your constant companion, I would offer support. Aid in any trouble that arrived. The two of us, having trained together, would pair well and provide confidence in your safe return." The rehearsed response was impressive.

Orin swished his hands through the water, removing the tidbits of plankton attached to his palms. Then he turned to give his friend his complete focus. "This means that much to you, Pauric?"

Pauric's smile indicated he knew a win was at hand for his campaign. While Orin had no desire to go to the surface world, he would for this man who had been by his side for years, never failing to come to his aid.

"Yes, Orin, it does. I only need you to say yes." Pauric spoke slowly, but bright eagerness lit up his face.

Orin laughed, shaking his head. "Fine, understand I do this for you, but when it is time to return, I will, with or without you."

This time, Pauric laughed. "Of course, my friend. Now, when shall we meet with your grandfather?"

"That is easier said than done."

"Well, what are we waiting for, then?"

Chapter Two

"You'll never get what you want by settling, Gavin," Coralia Hali said while popping carrots into her mouth at the bar.

"Shh, he might hear you." Gavin Dennehy smiled toward his date for the evening, who raised his glass back with a sweet smile. Gavin prepared to wrap up his tables since he had Tony's permission to leave early. "Bob is a nice guy. He has a great job. He enjoys reading—"

"Oh, wait! Let me! Let me!" Coralia pounced. "He enjoys walks on the beach. He's the perfect prospect boyfriend." She popped another carrot into her mouth and leaned her chin on a raised fist.

Gavin sighed. "Yes, Coralia. He does, or at least he says so. I'm not sure yet. We're getting to know each other."

"And I get that, but when you describe this poor delusional creature who thinks he's going to get in your pants tonight, he sounds like an ad for an elderly dating app and not someone you honestly want."

No one could accuse Coralia of not speaking her mind, but Gavin wanted safe, and Bob was safe.

"And how do you know what I want? I like him." Or at least he liked his profile. This would be their first date, and sure, there wasn't a brewing inferno in his balls for this guy, but who needed that? Gavin didn't. Nice, calm, and ordinary was what he was looking for as he cautiously dipped his toe into the dating scene again.

"Yes, Gavin, I can see that you do. But do you *want* him? There's not an ounce of heat in your eyes when you look at that kind and boring man over there."

Thankfully, Coralia didn't point a carrot toward Gavin's date for the evening, but her gaze did flicker the man's way.

"I don't need heat." Gavin had heat once, fire, and it burned him. No more burns for him. He was going to date Ted. Wait. Carl. No, Bob. His name was Bob, and he was going to enjoy it. Unfortunately for Bob, despite Coralia's observation, there wouldn't be anyone getting into Gavin's pants that evening, even if it seemed like forever since Gavin got any action.

He still had another hour to work, so he refilled Coralia's glass before leaving to check his tables. He enjoyed his job at Iliona's Safe Haven, where he'd worked as a waiter for the last few years. Tony, the manager, was friendly yet firm. He appreciated that Tony ran a tight ship but was compassionate and fair. He also enjoyed the family atmosphere, especially with Tony's children visiting daily. And while Tony was easy on the eyes, his husband, Adamaris, was a thing of beauty. Gavin enjoyed watching the pair, seeing what it was to love someone and have that love returned rather than tremble in fear of what might lurk within the shadows of a broken mind.

But he was safe now. There were no more shadows except for the ones he cast himself. He'd left no trace for Riordan to follow him, disappearing into the night the moment he'd had a chance to escape. Finally, after years of nothing, he could breathe, and with that, he was allowing himself to have a life. It was time.

Gavin glanced at Bob. Was a guy he'd met online, the hotbed of the dating world — well, at least Gavin's world — the ideal candidate? He seemed nice, he was quiet, and he had a sweet smile. So that made Bob a safe bet, which was what Gavin wanted.

How many times had he regretted giving Riordan his heart, submitting to him only for the man — who swore to protect him — to end up hurting him so severely later? Riordan blamed the drugs, the pills, and powders he took to achieve the robust frame, which he'd later used to pummel

Gavin nearly to death the last time. But Riordan had chosen to take them, even though he admitted that the stuff he was using to get bigger to achieve his weight class as a boxer was changing him, making him angrier. Had that stopped him? No. He continued to use them, getting more hostile until he couldn't control his bouts of rage.

In one of the last violent encounters Gavin had experienced with his ex, Gavin had made the unfortunate choice to cook chicken instead of fish. Riordan had accused him of sabotaging his meal plan and unleashed his fury. The man who had claimed to love him shouted at him with each brutal blow, calling him a stupid bitch, and screaming at him to leave. It took two of their next-door neighbors to break in and pull Riordan off of him. Gavin had blacked out, bruised, bloody, and broken, and woke in the emergency room where the doctor had diagnosed a concussion.

Welp, that had been the turning point for Gavin. After he left the hospital, he snuck into the apartment he'd shared with Riordan—who had become his abusive prison warden—packed his shit, and took off. Unfortunately his escape had been short-lived because Riordan had found him a few days later and dragged him back to his cell. Riordan's parents were apparently excellent at using their money to find their son's wayward toy.

When he'd escaped the last time, remaining hidden the first year had been challenging. He jumped at sudden noises, timid as a mouse. He'd moved into a small apartment and found a job washing dishes before moving up the chain to a server. The tips he got working at Iliona's Safe Haven helped pay the few bills he incurred.

In addition, the food his boss made sure he took home helped him gain a little weight, so he looked less like a skeleton wrapped in paper-thin skin and more like the dancer he used to be.

Sadly, Gavin could no longer be the dancer he'd been in the past. He refused to do anything to help Riordan find him. The boy who had dazzled audiences around the globe no longer existed. He still yearned for his dancing life and even considered giving dance classes for kids, but that was out of the question. There undoubtedly would be a mother or father who knew of Gavin Dennehy, the dancer who had thrilled thousands. No, he was happy as Gavin, the server, no one of significance.

And that *Gavin is glad to be going on a date with Bob.*

"Oh, I see that look." Coralia broke into his musing. "That's one of those *I accept my fate* looks. Of course, it's whatever you want to do, but—Holy fuck!"

Gavin was startled from his task of refilling silverware and looked at Coralia. He followed her gaze across the restaurant as a pair of men entered the door. Gavin didn't know which one had caught her attention, but he certainly knew which one had grabbed his eye, and there was no way he was going anywhere near the guy.

The man stood tall with gorgeously dark skin, contrasting with his white-blond locs that hung in twisted coils down his back. He wore a rust-colored sweater wrapped around well-shaped muscles. Gavin felt like he'd been struck by lightning and found it hard to look away. Then, as if he'd called to the guy, the man turned, searching until his gaze locked on Gavin.

"Fuck is right." Of course he'd whispered it to himself so the yummy eye candy wouldn't hear him. Yet why did the man suddenly smile at him as if he had? And why did Gavin hold his breath until he forced himself to look away?

"I've never seen hair quite that color before." Coralia sighed.

No, Gavin hadn't, either. It was almost a golden silver, shimmering in the restaurant's lights.

"I mean, it's like a rich coppery red. Is that shine even possible? I guess if it were dyed, it could be, but it seems natural. And look at his shoulders. I could very happily climb that man."

Clearly, he and Coralia were not staring at the same man. That was a good thing. But wait . . . It didn't matter, because Gavin didn't care. The one Coralia was salivating over was equally tall with a twin set of buff shoulders, a wide chest, and an easy laugh. He strode confidently, gesturing around the restaurant as if seeing it for the first time.

Gavin knew Iliona's Safe Haven was a sight to take in. Framed pictures of sea creatures hung on the walls, displayed as if they were family members. The carved wooden bar showed ocean waves wrapped around its body, giving it movement. Lights illuminated it from the floor, giving it lovely shadowing. The chandeliers above it were stained glass with an octopus sliding his impressive tentacles along.

The tables circled out from the bar, and diners sat comfortably in wide chairs to cushion their bottoms. The restaurant welcomed visits, long chats, and family time. So many of the same clients repeatedly returned, sharing stories and tales. Gavin sometimes stopped to listen, hearing fantastic stories boasting interesting imaginings of mermen, sea creatures, and adventures.

The casual atmosphere provided a welcome change from living in New York. The hustle and bustle, the constant hurry was absent here, and Gavin loved it.

Gavin glanced at the men again, surprising himself at how quickly he envisioned kneeling at the darker man's feet, the man's hand tugging at Gavin's longish hair. He hadn't worried about trimming his hair in ages, but to feel those fingers on his scalp would be a plus for keeping the long strands.

The fantasy of his heart was to be loved and owned. To be

possessed by another to whom he could freely and fully submit. Perhaps that was one of the things about his relationship with Riordon that he'd fought the most. His ex-boyfriend wanted power. He wanted control. He wanted Gavin to be obedient to his every whim. Yet no matter how intense and overwhelming Riordan was, Gavin refused to completely yield. He never felt safe enough to fully trust Riordan. Unfortunately, his mistrust proved to be accurate.

Now look at him, focusing on this stranger instead of working. He needed to finish work and not join Coralia fantasizing about a man, especially when he had a guy he planned to go out with that very night. How disrespectful of him when he had every intention to enjoy an evening with Ted. Wait . . . Michael? Reuban? Shit. Bob. The man's name was Bob. When Gavin tore his gaze away from the one who'd almost captured his soul by simply walking in, he saw Bob glancing from him to the stranger and back again.

Gavin gave Bob an awkward smile and spun around, picking up the silverware tray to carry the finished sets to the drawer.

"Hey, I see you running away. Tell me you didn't notice the gorgeous desserts over there." Coralia's voice sounded huskier than earlier, a sure sign of her interest in said desserts.

"Didn't see a thing," Gavin sing-songed as he put the sets away.

Gavin spent the rest of his time refilling Bob's water glass and avoiding the corner where the two men sat.

But no matter where he went, he felt the intensity of the stranger watching him. It gave him delicious chills that were all the more incentive to stay away.

Bob planned to take him bowling. It would be a risk-free outing with a safe man, and that was exactly what Gavin wanted.

He needed safe. He did not need to be bent over a chair,

laid on a table like a feast, or anything with a flat surface while that beautiful man did things to him.

The end of his shift finally arrived, and he clocked out and headed toward Bob with a smile.

"Ready?" Bob asked, straightening his tie.

"For you, anytime."

Well, that had a bit of flair, right?

Gavin accepted Bob's hand as he led him out of the restaurant. He ignored Coralia as he passed. Besides, her gaze was locked on her prey and the man who made him feel like one.

Chapter Three

"Did you see that?" Orin asked, moving his gaze from the fascinating man to glance at Pauric devouring the enormous amount of food he'd ordered. He lifted his fork with a heap of pasta and shellfish, consuming the bite and moaning over the delicious flavors.

"See what," Pauric asked after quickly swallowing yet another heaping forkful.

He dabbed at his lips with a cloth napkin before saying, "The man over there, a stunning work of art that's been watching me." He glanced at Pauric and winced. "And please slow down before you choke."

Orin shook his head. Pauric had enjoyed himself immensely since they'd arrived, trying every food imaginable. How ironic that his friend's favorites tended to include delicacies from their home. They were here to broaden their experiences and see what the surface world offered. Yet what drew them the most were things reminding them of home.

Orin had considered visiting the aquarium, one of the few places to pique his curiosity, but had hesitated. It would probably pale in comparison to what he knew and treasured at home, so maybe visiting the place wasn't the best idea.

"Sure it's not the other way around, my friend?" Pauric pointed his chin toward the object of Orin's attention. "Your gaze has followed him quite a bit since we've been here. I've been watching."

"Oh? You've noticed while you've scarfed down enough to feed a corps of Guardians." Orin picked up his glass and sipped the fizzy drink. Root beer. It was one of his favorite pleasures while here on the surface world. He found the way it tickled his nose enjoyable.

"Don't mind my stomach. You know I enjoy a good meal." Pauric polished off his plate just as Tony — mate to Adamaris, son of Lindh, who had mated Orin's brother Trillion — arrived at their table. Pauric pointed to the dessert he wished to try on the menu.

"Good choice." Tony nodded, patted Pauric's shoulder, and signaled to a server to secure Pauric's next culinary victim.

Trillian had recommended that Orin and Pauric visit the establishment his mate had created for their people, a sanctuary for mer. But then, how many thousands of years had man of land and sea crossed paths both on the surface and beneath the ocean's crests? How many humans needed rescue while seeking experiences to ease their boredom, trying to discover the joy of the ocean known to sea brothers and sisters for generations?

Likewise, so many beneath the waves had become fascinated with the mysteries of the surface world — the very reason Orin and Pauric were here.

"Do you plan to try everything on the menu?" Orin raised a brow.

"Well, who knows how long we'll be here? Unfortunately, someone failed to secure the date we must return. I, for one, will be enjoying every moment available to me until that day occurs." Pauric smiled happily when the server set a chocolate menagerie before him. He dug in, his sigh sounding very much like sex.

"You should be thankful. We 're here without a time limit. Nothing I do is without purpose." Orin took a spoon and sampled the dish, finding it enjoyable but perhaps not as much as Pauric. He appreciated the artistic touch of the plating, though, and had no doubt his brother Trillian, as an artist, had a hand in designing the preparation.

"Hm. Nicely done. Or, the way your grandfather is, we

could be here today and gone tomorrow," Pauric said, picking up a glass of water to wash down the dessert, disappearing at record speed.

Orin laughed. "One would think you haven't eaten in decades, my friend."

"Well, we wouldn't want such deliciousness to go to waste, would we?" Pauric dropped his napkin on the dish and pushed back from the bar top before eyeing the bread dish between them.

"With you, that is not even a remote possibility." Orin slid the rest of the bread over to Pauric.

Pauric picked one out, wolfing it down without remorse. Then he paused, his gaze on something across the room, the decimation of edible conquests forgotten.

Orin followed the direction of Pauric's gaze, smiling when he found what captured his friend's focus and slowed the destruction of the breadbasket.

"Who is that?" Pauric wiped his mouth and turned, fully taking in the woman standing next to the mouthwatering vision who had captured Orin's attention.

"Not sure, but she seems to know that man well."

Pauric glanced at him and then back at the pair. "Oh. I see now."

"Yes, I noticed him the moment we entered." No way Orin could have missed those broad shoulders and the long, shapely frame. How could anyone not immediately cease what they were doing the moment those thick, heavy, sunstruck curls came into view, complementing the grey eyes Orin could see from where he sat. And the lovely ass that teased him as the young man raced back and forth, completing his tasks, made him hungry to grab the roundness and leave his handprints on the set of superb cheeks.

"Well, then. I'm surprised you're still here berating my eating habits when you could be there acquiring your tasty morsel." Pauric wiped his hands, obviously done with his meal now that he had better things in view. He nodded to the server, who deftly picked up the meal's remains and walked away, then he tossed a few bills on the table and stood.

"Going to head over and try your luck?" Orin asked.

"Yes, Tetra Orin, I am. As well you should."

Unfortunately, Orin had seen the look of interest from the human at the other end of the bar. He'd also noticed the touches between the two as the young man passed.

"No, he is taken. At least for now." He wasn't one to interfere in the relationships of others, no matter how entranced he was.

Instead, he returned his friend's nod and watched Pauric approach the young woman. She looked up, tracking Pauric, curiosity in purple eyes that were both exquisite and familiar.

Doesn't Lindh have purple eyes?

He'd learned little of the merman since Trillian had returned with him. His brother was not known for sharing and had kept his new mate mostly to himself. However, he had learned that Lindh had twins from a previous mating with a mermaid who had been killed tragically. To lose the life of any merbeing was an incredible loss, but to lose one's mate? To survive afterword was unfathomable.

In fact, the more Orin observed his friend's target, the more like Lindh the woman appeared. But could this young lady be his brother's daughter, Lindh's blood child? He'd never met her, having been off training when Adamaris bonded with Tony. Still, she did very much favor Adamaris, whom he'd seen with Tony a few times while he and Pauric had been eating.

If this woman was Adamaris's sister, then he would have to gain an introduction and welcome her to their world.

But rather than focusing on Pauric and his hopeful conquest, Orin found himself refocusing on the young man who exited with his companion.

Where would they go?

Would they have sex?

Would the little urchin who had been salivating over the human Orin strongly wished for himself truly treasure the man the evening had gifted him?

Sighing, Orin picked up his root beer and sipped it, enjoying what he had in his possession rather than what he did not.

He glanced back at Pauric, who'd already engaged his young lady in a conversation. He could sense a strong indication of where things were going, given her smiles and the obvious warmth between the two.

Should Orin be jealous of Pauric's carefree take on relationships? Envy Pauric's ability to see what he wanted and take the plunge?

Orin had reasons for his careful steps. A Man of Neptune, son of Neptune's daughter, and a leader of Guardians, he couldn't just play where he wished. Besides, he had specific requirements, ones where his control and domination ruled.

He carefully chose who to bed and who he allowed in his life. Not everyone could appreciate the strong hand of an even stronger man.

And he required focus. Beautiful, compelling distractions didn't always fit in his world, no matter how much he greatly desired them.

"A lot on your mind there, Orin," Tony said before refilling his drink. "We'll have to keep you well-cupped with your root beer. Now, what's on your mind?"

"Nothing worth wasting your time with, I'm afraid."

"Okay. I'll be back in a few." Tony moved on to help other customers.

No, Orin wouldn't regale Tony with his tales of woe. That would be whining rather than enjoying the time his grandfather had granted him. Still, it wasn't as if he wanted to be here. He would have been happier taking care of his coral garden. Now, he sat wondering and questioning, remembering a graceful frame and soft gray eyes.

A state he rarely found himself in.

And it was entirely Pauric's fault.

"Another root beer, Orin?"

Orin gazed at Tony, his newly discovered nephew. The man was a good human, one Adamaris had seen and perhaps loved the moment they met. Could that sort of thing happen to Orin? Not likely. Orin didn't foresee a forever love for himself.

Why?

He wasn't a terrible person. He was a loving brother and an excellent leader. He was a loyal friend. He was desirable.

He knew the reason lay in his inability to share himself fully with another individual. If he were honest, it was his fear to do so. In the past, things had taken a turn for the worse once he allowed someone to glimpse who he truly was and what he desired in a relationship. He'd always ended the attempt before someone got hurt, physically or otherwise, including himself.

While pain could be a joy, it was only to be performed or received responsibly. It was to be treasured. And he'd yet to find the person who could accept the pain and love he could offer.

"I believe I've had enough, Tony, but your care is appreciated."

Tony nodded, placing a glass of water before him. "Plans for the night?"

Orin shook his head. "No, I prefer an evening in what is to be my home for however long I am here."

"You know, I'm not a merperson, and my grandfather certainly wasn't a mythical god, but it seems like your family goes through a great deal to acquire time to visit here. Yet I can't think of one evening you haven't spent at home."

Orin smiled — Tony was right. Pauric had tried to drag him out to no avail. He agreed to visit, but honestly? His coral garden was not here, and he found nothing to compare. He missed his home, missed the things that gave him comfort.

But then, had he tried? Or was he indeed acting like the exile Pauric had accused him of being?

"You're correct."

Tony nodded. "You know, one of the qualities of managing a restaurant is knowing the roles required and being able to fill each and every one. For example, I often find myself in the role of bartender most evenings. And do you know what bartenders often do?" For emphasis, he slid a thick cloth along the bar's surface, polishing it while staring at him intently.

"No, but I'm certain you will share this with me momentarily."

Tony laughed, the sound rich and warm. "Well, we listen. Not sure what equivalent you may have in Atlantis . . . maybe a counselor or therapist? Someone to talk to, share your problems with, your worries, breakups, and all that? But many bartenders have acted as a sounding board, a cheap therapist. You drink, talk, and we listen."

Orin shrugged. Well, for concerns or worries, he typically turned to Pauric. However, having someone else to listen and help sort his thoughts wouldn't hurt.

Tony leaned forward on one elbow. "Here we are. Mind telling me why you stay home? Scared?"

Orin laughed, the sound rusty to his ears. "Scared. I fear nothing here, Tony. I have lived my entire life as someone to be feared, trained to overcome any foe, outthink any obstacle."

Tony nodded. "All of that, huh? Well then, it shouldn't be a problem for you to go out and have some fun. See the place. Explore before you return home."

Orin leaned back in his seat, the hefty stool creaking beneath his girth. Folding his arms, he studied Tony. "And where would you suggest I explore?"

Tony rubbed his chin thoughtfully. "I may have a few ideas."

Chapter Four

Gavin sighed. *Red flags. Big, dark, and mysterious.*
Sure, Orin—because he now had the guy's name—was undeniably gorgeous with his silver twisted locs twined with gems, colorful beads, and shells. Plus, the man was incredibly tall with thick, sinewy muscles that Gavin mentally salivated over each evening when Orin returned to the restaurant. How many times had Gavin stumbled carrying a tray or setting a glass down, too focused on his boss's uncle to walk like a normal person?

As if he were a normal person . . .

What normal person was constantly attracted to dangerous men, men who could easily control him, manipulating his frame in just the positions they wanted to dominate him completely?

And he really wanted to be dominated.

Craved it, actually. Drugging, skin-on-skin friction. Touches that bruised, leaving marks that lasted days, reminding him of being taken.

Gavin wanted that.

But he'd never found what he longed for. His needs were too much for his partner, or the person bordered on a crazy that was hard to escape. Like his ex.

Riordan's crazy had sent him packing, moving to another state. He'd left behind a career he'd studied for, earned a degree and even a master's, but had been forced to desert. Fleeing far and fast as if his life depended on it. Because in the end, it had.

No, he couldn't make himself try again. No matter that Orin looked at him every evening with so much dominance that it made him almost want to plead for more. The man was just this side of perfection, the one he'd dreamed of for so

21

long.

No.

Snapping out of it, he went back to wrapping silverware.

"Can you bend metal with the power of your mind? Your thoughts appear so intense it would not surprise me. Your glance burns, and I find that I like the heat." The breath from whispered words skated over his ear.

Gavin shivered. He knew, without turning, exactly who stood close to him, the more massive frame aligning with his perfectly.

He reminded himself to breathe before turning around, taking in Orin standing before him with a mischievous look.

"You are so focused. I find myself envious," Orin murmured. "It would please me greatly to be the recipient of such attention."

Gavin could melt right there for all to see. This man's words and presence saturated the entire space around him, becoming his whole world. Orin's sexy voice made him hungry to act out fantasies he'd had lying in his bed alone. Being next to the man was a dream. All-encompassing and delicious.

What's he like in bed?

Gavin couldn't help but wonder . . . . He wasn't a little guy like men Orin's size usually favored. Men who were spritely, lithe creatures who haunted clubs Gavin never felt comfortable in.

Could Orin accept that Gavin loved being held down . . . controlled . . . manhandled? Hmm . . . He rarely got what he desired so badly his teeth ached.

Gavin awkwardly cleared his throat, easing forward and nearly moaning when Orin moved with him. "Uhm. I thought you were talking to your nephew." He shivered at having Orin so close to him. He'd imagined this, dreamed of it. And now that he had it, his nerves were taking over.

"I would much rather talk to you. I tire of not taking what

I want, Gavin."

Taking what he wanted? Did Orin want him?

Hearing Orin utter his name gave Gavin chills. How often had he lied to himself, thinking he'd mastered his body's reactions to the man?

No, he hadn't mastered it. Instead, he'd created an emptiness only the man himself could satisfy. He'd fantasized, huge Orin-shaped fantasies of what this man could do to him. He imagined himself on his knees, mouth wrapped around what promised to be a sizeable cock. He hoped for welts up and down his back, striping his ass with visible marks lasting for days.

Marks Gavin would trace and cherish.

He wanted this man to give him those things.

Gavin's date with Todd — or whatever his name was — had been a failed evening, and he never called the guy back. Instead of focusing on his date, thoughts of Orin had occupied his mind. And now Orin was crossing the barrier Gavin tried to erect.

One he needed to keep himself safe.

Orin's hand slid down Gavin's arm, grasping Gavin's fingers. Dragged against the man, Gavin sighed.

"Look at your beautiful eyes, such a unique shade of gray. Almost silver. It reminds me of the moon's light when it falls on the ocean's surface. When I rise, it captures me, just as seeing you, wanting you, has done for me." Orin kissed Gavin's ear, swiping his tongue over the skin just below.

Gavin shivered. "P-Poetry?"

"I've never been accused of flowery words, yet I find myself inspired." Reaching behind him, Orin withdrew a snow globe.

Gavin looked within to see an ocean scene with coral beds brilliantly arrayed while fish swam around. It was beautiful, but he had no idea why Orin had chosen to share this with him. He would rather have more of his touches and revel in more kisses.

He looked up to see Orin staring at him.

"Life is very like the scene in this water vessel." Orin swirled the globe, twisting it about. "It requires balance. Outside of ourselves, some factors may shake our existence, unsettling us. But we must look within for hope, for a second chance to begin again."

Gavin watched, mesmerized by the man's voice as the chaos within the globe calmed.

"And then we find ourselves settled. We took a chance. We tried. We moved beyond our fears. And we survive, greater than we were before." Orin placed the globe in Gavin's hand.

Gavin should have stopped him, should have pulled back and away. He didn't, though. He welcomed Orin's warm lips against his. Sharp teeth nipping him made him moan, eager as a bitch in heat.

Orin moved away, but Gavin followed, desperate for more.

"Shh. I have you," Orin murmured. "Tonight, we will leave here together. No more games. No more running."

"I haven't been playing games. I don't do that." Gavin didn't hide from the truth. No, he'd been protecting himself from this very thing, this blazing attraction to a man who would cause a fiery inferno to erode his senses.

"But you have been running."

He had. That was true. And he couldn't promise he wouldn't keep doing it. "I had to."

"No more. Tell me you accept this, accept a possible us, because I know you feel this, feel what we could be." Orin placed his palm against Gavin's heart.

Gavin stared into Orin's eyes, his pulse pounding rapidly, and whispered, "I'm afraid."

"You should be. You should be terrified of the way I want you, how much I want you. The way I crave seeing your eyes wet with tears, hearing my name shouted from your lips. The way I wish to be your focus . . . to own you. But you can't keep yourself away from me, from this anymore."

Gavin closed his eyes, leaning against the man before him, savoring the embrace.

He detected no lies from the man and no over-the-top promises. From what he'd heard when Orin spoke with Tony and Adamaris. he could tell there was an honesty to Orin, a sincerity he'd wished for in others. Years ago, he'd hoped for that in Riordan, and it had cost him bits of his soul that had taken time to get back and still more lost forever.

Could he risk himself again? Could he give him and Orin a chance?

There would be no more hiding the truth of his need from Orin. Gavin had lied to himself, thinking that the way he watched and followed him with his soul crying out had gone unseen.

No, Orin had seen it all and finally come to claim him.

"I don't know what happened to make you afraid. I can feel your heart racing." Orin wrapped his hand around Gavin's throat, his thumb pressed against his Adam's apple, making it difficult to breathe. "But that has nothing to do with here and now. Those fears should not be allowed to impair an opportunity for happiness. What matters is us and what we need from each other."

Gavin swallowed, his life in Orin's hands, and he had never felt safer. His breathing slowed, his gaze locked on Orin.

"There you are, beautiful creature. Focus on me."

"Gavin, are you okay?" Jenny, one of the other servers, asked.

Gavin nodded, his gaze never leaving Orin's.

"Okay," she muttered as she walked away, her tone unsure.

Gavin couldn't give her reassurances when Orin had his complete focus.

"When you leave here tonight, you will be with me, remembering what we can be for each other. You need to understand that I mean to keep you."

Orin kissed him again, and he fell deeply into the moment, drowning in the need washing over him.

"Nod yes, Gavin."

Gavin nodded, and his eyes filled with tears.

"Good. Very good."

Gavin whimpered when Orin thrust a fist into his curls, yanking his head back roughly. Twin sharp points skewered into his neck, and he could swear he heard Orin swallow.

Hidden away in the restaurant's corner, could anyone hear his gasp?

Moments later, Orin's tongue lapped against the pinpricks of pain.

Gavin staggered against Orin, but the man quickly righted him, holding him tightly before he walked away.

In a daze, Gavin stared after Orin, who sat back at the bar, talking to Tony while keeping an eye on him.

Gavin shivered, returning to work after having his world rocked in the best way possible.

"So, plans for tonight?" Jenny whispered, surprising him into a startled bark of surprise. She laughed.

Gavin felt his cheeks warm. "Maybe."

"Oh, I'm thinking it's more a *definitely*. Be careful playing with that one. He looks dangerous."

Gavin had to stop himself from licking his lips in anticipation. "I'll be careful, Jenny. Thanks."

Gavin appreciated the few friends he had. For a while he'd refused to build ties after he'd moved, too afraid that someone or something would lead Riordan to him. But Jenny and Coralia had wormed their way into his heart, slipping beneath the fortress he'd built around himself. He had quickly learned he could depend on them to have his back after being alone for so long.

He and Jenny had met when they'd interviewed at the restaurant on the same day. When they both got the job, fate had them becoming close friends. Jenny took it upon herself to look out for him, helping to keep the crazies away. His wingman for life?

"Uhm. He's nice?" Yes, he posed it as a question because Orin wasn't nice. He seemed just as dangerous as Jenny warned. Yet how could he explain to his friend that Orin's style of danger was what got his blood thrumming to life?

As he delivered drinks to his latest table, he glanced at Orin and found him watching his every move.

"Nice, huh?" Jenny asked when he returned to the bar. "The looks that man's throwing you have nothing to do with nice." She hip-checked him before moving swiftly to take a couple's order.

Gavin laughed. Well, Gavin's date with Bob had been *nice*, but what had that done for him? It made his dick limp for one. He had to be honest with himself. Nice didn't do anything for him, but he didn't want to die for what he truly wanted, either.

How dangerous was Orin? Where did he come from? His family? Gavin knew Tony was part of that family and that Tony was married to Adamaris. But there had been no mention of anyone else except Orin's friend Pauric, who appeared fascinated by Coralia.

Pauric and Coralia had become inseparable. Coralia, his unflappable friend, smiled brightly whenever Pauric was near. And Pauric? He glowed with her attention. Gavin was a little envious of what they shared.

He wanted that, had been denying it, torturing himself too long. If he could have even a little of what he saw Coralia

embracing, why shouldn't he?
     Fears be damned.

Chapter Five

Orin barely registered Tony's words as he watched Gavin struggle to regain his balance. That effortless grace he usually wore as he moved from table to table appeared more challenging for him to acquire. Orin smiled, knowing he was responsible for throwing Gavin off balance.

Do I regret it? Absolutely not.

Making a dent in Gavin's fortress walls excited Orin. So many nights he'd spent at the bar, spearing the man with his gaze, trying to capture the elusive manta ray. He'd even tried to engage him in conversation, to no avail. Gavin deftly evaded him each time but tracked him, the heat from his fiery gaze a siren's call to Orin's need to tame.

Orin grew tired of waiting for Gavin to come to him since he wasn't sure how much time he had left before he would be summoned to return home. His grandfather hadn't given him a designated time, and Orin hadn't pressed him for it.

From the moment he spotted Gavin, he'd appreciated the time and would even more if he could capture his prey. He had just confirmed Gavin's reciprocating desires but sensed his unwavering hesitation. Perhaps that was the reason Neptune had gifted him with what appeared to be unlimited time.

Surprisingly, Pauric had been correct about Orin needing this time. More so than he would ever admit to his friend.

Watching how Gavin's gaze flitted toward him and away made him want the man more than he needed to breathe. Gavin was exquisite, tall but shorter than him, and wide enough to grip and spin to meet his desires without worry of damaging him. Gavin wasn't like the slim creatures he'd often played with. No, this man, this human, was strong and powerful. And yet he displayed a vulnerability and a gentle soul, waiting for the right person to take him in hand.

That person would be Orin.

The way Gavin had melted against him, his eyes soft and warm, Orin easily detected the man's eagerness for touch and possession.

Orin didn't just want to show Gavin his world, the hint he'd shared through a water vessel. No, when he returned, he wouldn't be traveling alone. Somehow, he would convince Gavin to come with him. They would live in what would be their world together.

His brothers had each found their mates, their treasures.

Can it now be my turn?

"Here again, friend?" Pauric said as he eased his bulk onto the stool beside Orin's.

Orin was surprised to see Pauric. He'd seen less of his friend since the man had begun his pursuit of the lovely Coralia. He couldn't blame Pauric. Coralia was a sweet creature who watched after those in her charge, from the young of Tony and Adamaris to those she called friends. Pauric could not have chosen a more equal mate. He didn't envy him having to return alone should the female not deign to accompany him.

He, however, refused to suffer that fate. "I am."

"And so?" Pauric said, accepting a drink from Tony, who smiled at him knowingly.

"Girl's night leave you lonely, Pauric?" Tony laughed.

Pauric laughed as well. "Have to let the woman breathe sometime, I suppose. It appears I'm unable to compete with what your daughter offers."

Tony smiled. "Yes, well, this has been a long-standing event for the girls. An annual festival where they shop, buying lots of pretty things and art supplies, then a meal and a movie. It's been that way for the last few years."

Pauric nodded solemnly. "I would never interfere with this time that they both need."

Tony smiled. "Yes, Coralia finds her motherly and sometimes sisterly instincts fed by my daughter, who needs both. I'm grateful for her and rather protective, I might add."

Orin held his tongue as he listened to the human verbally circle the merman—a hunter fairly familiar with the art of subterfuge.

"I am as well." Pauric glared at Tony, his golden amber eyes flinty and hard. Prepared for battle.

Tony nodded, apparently seeing what he sought. "Good. Sounds very good. I would hate for anyone to believe that Coralia's heart is a toy to play with."

"That I would never do, I can assure you, Tony." Pauric kept his gaze steady.

Tony stared a moment longer before he smiled and slid a menu to Pauric.

Orin shook his head at them both and turned, choosing instead to search out his beauty.

"So, Orin? How are we coming along?" Pauric picked up the menu, reading over the choices. As Tony liked to change things up, a diner could always find something new and flavorful.

"Progressing."

"Yes, if the blush we can all see from here is to be believed." Tony nodded to where Gavin stood, still sneaking looks at Orin.

It did much for Orin's pride to have the man of his dreams watch him, wanting him even if said man was shy about his desires.

It only made Orin hunger for him more.

"Yes, and it's a lovely shade. A color I shall hopefully see spread all over his enticing frame later, perhaps even this evening." Orin could picture it now.

"Whoa. Too much information." Tony held out his hand. "But I am happy for you. The near stalking you've been

31

doing? Pitiful. At least you're getting somewhere now." He turned to answer a question on the types of pints he offered, taking an order before returning to Orin and Pauric.

Orin noticed the disappointed look of the urchin at the bar, who no doubt thought folding his thick arms to present his inked muscles would capture Tony's attention. Orin could only shake his head. No, Tony only had eyes for Adamaris. Orin felt the same regarding Gavin. Nothing else and no one else mattered.

"Yes, now I only need to determine where to take my conquest. I want Gavin to see what matters to me, my world. It's not time, though. I went for a smaller scale."

"The snow globe?" Pauric interjected. "He liked it?"

Orin remembered the smile on Gavin's face and the taste of his flesh. He recalled how Gavin had grasped the globe tightly, like a treasured possession. "Yes, Pauric. It made a lovely impression. Now, I need to think about this evening, something that would move me closer to my goal."

"Hm, and would that goal be taking him to your home?" Tony paused to answer a question from the same young man. He was professional and kind, the perfect restauranteur, but still not reacting as the boy wished.

Orin smiled and went back to watching his future mate. "Of course. He's mine and should return home with me."

"If he wants to. Perhaps he will choose to stay here." Pauric stared at him, no doubt gauging his response.

It wasn't as if Orin hadn't considered that possibility. It was a worry, honestly. Still, he felt confident he could convince his mate that *his* home would be the best place for them.

"Yes, Orin, I, too, would like to take my lovely Coralia home, but should she decide to stay, I will remain with her. I am not as important to Neptune as you are. But you, my friend, have decisions to make, which cannot be made alone or without thinking of the people you lead. It would also be best to allow Gavin to make his own choices, which you may not like. Ultimately, it'll be worth it for a life and love with no regrets."

Pauric was right. He would have to be completely clear with Gavin. No relationship begun with secrets was one to last. Yet his secrets and the fact that he was not human but a merperson could be challenging to accept.

It would require some consideration.

"The aquarium," Tony said after dropping off a drink to another diner.

"The aquarium?" Orin asked.

Tony refilled a dish with sweet candies. "Yes, while it is not a true portrayal of life beneath the surface, it will help the conversations you need with him. You can assess Gavin's fears and interests."

Orin gave it some thought. A visit to the aquarium might be what they needed. An ease into the life his Gavin would share with him. It would be a start, at least.

Searching out his soon-to-be mate, Orin felt a wave of unease wash over him. Seeing Gavin bustling about, his strong body administering to the restaurant's needs, he was comforted to find him safe. Still, there was something just beyond his periphery, something that bore watching.

"You sense something, brother?" Pauric asked, glancing about, immediately becoming the soldier he'd trained to be, his body poised to engage any unseen enemy.

Pauric's shift would have been humorous if not for Orin's concern. There was something here, something out of place, possibly meaning harm. And because he felt it, Pauric, who knew him better than any of his brothers, recognized the sign of danger. His laughing, playful friend was not an easy opponent.

Pauric's attention helped settle Orin so he could send out

his energy, drifting it like fingers over each person in the restaurant. It was a skill he possessed, a gift from Neptune. He wasn't a siren like his brother Kamau, who possessed the gift of song affecting anyone who could hear, able to bring their souls to him. His gift was more a kinship with nature and living forms. It was why his coral garden called to him. He could sense it, and by sensing those around him, he could detect any dark energy that might lurk.

Pauric waited, shifting his weight to defend Orin. Orin nodded at him before closing his eyes and breathing in, sensing something there, someone hidden enough not to draw his full attention. He opened his eyes to gaze around the perimeter, certain that danger was present. When nothing stood out, he returned his focus to Gavin, who carried a steaming meal on a tray, gracefully ducking around other servers before placing it gently on a table a few feet from Orin.

Obviously aware of Orin's nearness, Gavin glanced his way, smiling nervously before speaking with the customers to assess their needs.

Orin wanted to go to him, sink his teeth into that long neck, and claim him before all present. Though claiming Gavin was chief among his list of things to accomplish, the uneasy feeling remained, placing his desires beneath a heavy shadow.

He stood, gathering his metaphysical armor about him, moving away from the bar, searching for whatever danger lurked nearby. Careful not to appear obvious, he examined each of the diners.

Was there one that focused on his future mate, on him? Perhaps it was all in his mind, his inability to leave his state of alertness at home in the sea.

Orin saw it then, a young human watching Gavin hungrily. Orin moved forward, intent on ending the creature that wanted his mate, stopping only when he felt a firm grasp on his elbow.

"Hold, friend. You have no trident to run him through, and killing him would draw attention. We cannot treat this world as we do our own."

Orin nearly growled, but Pauric was right. They were operating under different laws here. He ran his tongue over the sharp blades in his mouth, breathing deep until they reformed into the human equivalent, not that of a shifted mercreature prepared for battle.

He allowed Pauric to guide him back to the bar but remained aware of the unknown's presence.

Did his mate know the human? Who was this person?

The man turned his head, his watchful gaze falling on Orin.

Orin smiled, showing his teeth to challenge his enemy. A brow crease and a look of disdain were the only responses before the man stood, throwing some money at the table and exiting the restaurant.

"What was that about, my friend?"

Orin had no idea. He should have realized that obtaining what he'd dreamed of all his life would not come easily. Sure, he hadn't initially wanted to visit the surface world. He'd accepted his role as a Guardian, his purpose. Had he longed for something more? Perhaps, but he'd made do, forcing himself to accept there would be nothing more.

Now? Now, he'd met this beautiful human, unselfish and delectable. Gavin was Orin's reward for a life lived with focus and dedication. Gavin was his gift for every trial he'd survived, every battle won, and he was worth the wait.

Orin would not allow anyone, including the mysterious serpent slithering out of the exit, to deter him.

"What would you have me do, Tetra Orin?" Pauric whispered near his shoulder.

Hearing his title from his friend's lips forced Orin to take a deep breath. They were people of action, not ones to allow dangerous threats. Orin was no fool. If he saw Gavin's value, others did as well.

"Allow a moment and seek him out. Find out where he travels."

With a quick nod, Pauric was off, no doubt excited about his task.

"What's going on, warrior?" Coralia slipped into Pauric's place. "I saw the look Pauric wore on his way out to complete whatever secretive mission you sent him on. Before you deny it, I haven't known him long, but he's the other half of my soul. He clearly has a purpose and doesn't need to be distracted by my presence. But I know you have all the answers, beautiful man. Share."

Orin glanced at the creature beside him. She would make a formidable champion, a worthy Guardian, quick-witted yet graceful. Pauric had found a jewel, one he should never let go. Orin understood that as he looked at Gavin, remembering his sweet, shy smiles, the submission calling to Orin from his powerful frame. Orin had discovered his pearl, his treasure.

"There was another here, human, I think." Was he human?

"You're not sure."

"No, and I'm not certain if he noticed me observing him. He only saw Gavin."

"Ah, Gavin." Coralia watched Gavin for a moment, then turned back to Orin. "He's been through a lot."

"Has he?" Perhaps Orin could obtain a few answers, too. While he had enjoyed the small talks he and Coralia had shared, this one could prove more significant. She could tell him of his mate and aid him in providing a place of safety and security.

"Yes, he was in a dark place when he arrived. Afraid of his own shadow, jumpy. Of course, Tony and Adamaris drew him into their circle immediately. They tend to adopt the lonely and fearful. Just as they made a home for each other, they do their best to provide the same for those who wander in lost."

From what Orin had seen of the restaurant that took in many, she spoke the truth. The laughter, the shared stories, and the food passed to a hungry wanderer were easy to see. Even though Orin spent much of his adult life focused more on leadership and responsibility than the joy of fellowship and family, he recognized the gift Tony and Adamaris shared with others, one many appreciated.

"I understand."

"Do you, Orin? I see how you look at him as if he belongs to you."

"He does. He's mine." No question, no hesitation. Orin needed all who saw Gavin to know unmistakably that he was no longer an independent being but one who would be cherished and possessed by his mate.

Orin would extinguish anyone who dared to challenge his claim. To be this close to what he wished for most? No, Orin wouldn't allow anyone to take that from him. He would keep Gavin's heart safe and protected as well.

"Gavin is more than a thing for you to own. He has feelings, a history that existed long before you arrived. He will need the care Pauric said you are capable of as a merman tending to the needs of soldiers. Pauric says you are father and brother." Coralia's earnest expression bore into him. "Though he claims you sometimes dismiss this when you think of who you are and what you mean to others, but everyone who knows you sees it."

Orin nodded. His friend was right. When he considered words to describe himself, father to others never rose. But he had always watched over his people, cared for them and their families, and ensured all were supported and that no decision made put his people at unnecessary risk. Even during his time away, he opened the portal to check in, only to be told that all was well and that his coral beds were fine. Gideon had told him not to worry. Kasha had reminded him to enjoy his time away.

He smiled, their support filling him with warmth.

Coralia nodded. "There you are. That's the man Gavin needs to see, the one who looks both soft and strong, who can offer a safe place."

"I am not always soft nor tender. I am a soldier, a Guardian first and foremost."

Coralia gave him a sideways look. "That may be your perception, but I'm willing to believe there's more to you than you know. And who am I to say that Gavin couldn't use a little of your powerful leadership, too? Just remember . . . layers. We're all layers."

Layers like his coral beds, filled with layers of life and vegetation, an ecosystem astounding in its beauty.

He recalled her earlier words and asked, "Coralia, are you able to tell me more about these shadows? What brought Gavin here?"

Coralia sighed. "Unfortunately, that's not my story to tell."

"Even if it would help me keep him safe?"

Coralia considered it, her brow arched in thought. "I can't say much, only that there was an ex who seemed to be everything he wanted initially. Unfortunately, he started drinking and using drugs, which caused him to become violent. But he has a family with money and means, and for years, Gavin struggled to remain two steps ahead of them. When he got here, though, he found a safe place in this restaurant and with my family."

Orin nodded, settling in to listen.

Chapter Six

Gavin wondered what Coralia and Orin were discussing. The topic caused the big man to frown and look his way several times with concern.

It had to be about him. What was Coralia telling him? She was like an overprotective big sister sometimes. Having never had that, Gavin usually loved it. Right now? Not so much.

Gavin sighed. He was looking forward to spending time with Orin and getting to know him. And, well . . . he just wanted to be with the man. The moment they'd shared earlier hadn't been enough. He touched his neck, where he could feel the raised marks left behind. He wanted more of that.

He sighed when Coralia looked his way. But then she winked, and something settled in his chest.

Maybe it will be okay?

He had to admit he'd been craving someone like Orin.

Someone who could make him fall to his knees and beg.

He looked at Orin again, picturing those big hands lifting him, manipulating his body, forcing him to submit. It had been so long since anyone made him feel safe enough to even consider such possibilities. He grew hard with the thought and turned away.

"So you're going out with him," Jenny asked, bumping his hips with her own.

"Maybe."

"Okay. Remember, I warned you. You can't play games with this one."

"Games?"

"You know, games. Like people do."

Gavin wasn't playing games with anyone. Jenny didn't know him like that. What was she trying to say?

As if trying to smooth her words, she quickly added, "No

harm meant. Just you know, be careful." She winked before grabbing her tray and walking away.

Later, as Gavin prepared for his evening with Orin, he recalled Jenny's words.

Do I have expectations? Is Orin looking for more than I can give right now?

No, what he would not do was cause himself any stress by weaving someone else's hang-ups into his menagerie of anxiety. He had enough all by himself.

He looked in the mirror and didn't see the fit guy he used to be, with abs popping up whenever he moved. He was softer, his muscles not nearly as defined as when he'd been a swimmer during the summer and played football during the fall. Danced . . . Sure, he worked out, but he wasn't going to lie to himself, pretending his body was the thing of fantasies it might have been in the past.

He was tall, his hair curly, settling on his shoulders, the cut far past his norm. His eyes were gray. He'd say they were average like him, but even his last date had described them as bits of silver. Maybe that was what Orin saw, what attracted him.

Gavin touched his cheek, tracing his fingertips over the scar, an outward reminder of why he'd run so fast and far from home. Why he still sometimes felt like running.

He thought back to earlier in the day, remembering the chill he'd felt near the end of his shift. He'd shaken it off, but seeing the scar from what had healed on the outside but remained an open wound within, he couldn't ignore the shard of fear that it wasn't over. He'd promised himself he wouldn't be afraid anymore, that his past would no longer drive him. He wasn't stupid, though. His tormentor could be out there, somewhere, preparing to finish the job.

Unbidden images of his previous escape attempt came rushing forward. He had been staying in a run-down motel, working at a grocery store, feeding himself off expired food and leftovers he found here and there. When he wasn't working, he'd stayed in his dank room where the rain would wash insects under the door's crack on stormy nights.

For some reason, he hadn't hesitated when someone knocked on his door. For weeks, he'd been hungry, tired, and lonely but safe. Or so he thought.

"Trying to leave me, Gavin? You will never have a life without me. There's not a place you can go where I won't find you. My parents make sure I'm happy. They think you're perfect for me. I know you are. They'll do whatever's necessary to ensure you never get away."

Gavin could only gape at seeing Riordan standing there, the smell of marijuana strong enough that he should have recognized who had knocked before opening the door. Shocked to his core, his reaction time was too slow when Riordan backhanded him hard against his face. He'd fallen, his head striking the chair next to the door. The bags he carried — filled with expired groceries he'd hoped to cook that night — spilled across the floor.

In seconds, Riordan had his hands wrapped around Gavin's throat, yanking him to his feet and striking him again, the pain of the assault nearly blinding him.

"You fucking think you can leave me, bitch? You will always be mine. I own you, Gavin. Go ahead. Cry. No one around here cares. You chose the perfect place where I can teach you again who you belong to. And no one will call the police. I take care of you, give you everything, and this hell hole is where you keep yourself."

"Please, Riordan. Please." Gavin begged, pleading for his life.

But Riordan was right. No one came to help him.

No one cared.

Riordan quickly drove them back to the prison Gavin had shared with the man who promised to love him forever. Bloody and broken, he could only lie in the bed and wallow in misery.

Riordan's parents had improved the security system of Riordan's home, ensuring Gavin didn't have access. Fortunately, they underestimated both his spirit and their maid's kindness. Cori had little brothers, and no matter how much money the Drake family paid her to keep the home he shared with Riordan clean, she could not disregard Gavin's pain. Cori fed him, helped him gather his energy, and eventually aided him in escaping, directing him to a place where he could be safe and disappear.

And for five years, he'd lived here, secure without shadows of his past. The first year had been challenging, constantly checking for signs that Riordan had found him once again, always afraid. It had taken time, but he was no longer afraid to open doors, not worried if his former lover would appear to thrust him back into a living nightmare.

But there was that moment earlier, a feeling . . .

No. I will not do this again. I'm free. I'm not going back there. Not physically and not in my mind.

He didn't know what had happened to Riordan after he left. Maybe the drugs and the other crutches he'd used for pain, which had taken him over mind and body, had finally destroyed him. The man had become a monster, paranoid and horrific, hyper-focused on getting his pills and keeping Gavin a prisoner.

Gavin had tried to tell Riordan's parents of his behavior, but Allen and Barbara refused to listen to him, insisting that he was being ungrateful.

"Sometimes Riordan has little tantrums," Barbara had said after he showed her his black eye and split lip. "He'll be fine. Just give him what he wants. Keep him happy, and he won't hurt you." Her words were sharp, but similar shadows in her eyes whispered of hidden truths.

Gavin suspected Barbara had been living her own nightmare.

Should Gavin feel sorry for Riordan? For his family? For Barbara? Should he have done more to help the man he loved once?

No. Never.

Gavin sometimes missed the sweet person Riordan had been in the beginning. The man who shared walks with him in the park and talked of someday having children. The one who surprised him with fresh-cut flowers and breakfast in bed. He remembered those happier moments, but they hadn't lasted.

Gavin wouldn't live his life wishing for shattered dreams. Nope. This evening, he would go to the aquarium with Orin and leave himself open to possibilities.

Not quite ready for Orin to know where he lived, Gavin met him at the aquarium. Seeing Orin waiting for him with a look of hungry anticipation on his face nearly made Gavin ask to drop to his knees and swallow his dick down his throat. He barely held himself back.

Whew!

Gavin struggled to get his horny thoughts under control. Simply looking at Orin made him want to fall at the man's feet, let him rule his body, and possess him fully. The feeling was intense, overwhelming, and unlike anything he'd ever felt.

Taking a deep breath, he pressed forward, standing in front of Orin, daring to stare at the man's eyes.

"Thank you for this, Gavin. I have wished to see you outside of the restaurant. You here with me is a gift I will treasure."

Orin leaned forward, gently pressing his lips against Gavin's, then ending the kiss way too soon. Gavin licked his lips, sampling Orin's flavor and eager for another taste.

"You are delicious, so much heat." Orin slid a hand down Gavin's arm, pulling him against him, breathing in his scent.

Gavin had taken care to select one of his better colognes. He hoped Orin liked it.

He took Orin's offered hand, and they turned toward the building. Of course, they faced a large crowd, but Gavin didn't notice any of them, his attention entirely focused on the man beside him.

Orin stepped with the grace of someone who conserved movements. The man was huge, larger than Gavin, who wasn't a small man. And where he had grown soft in some places, he saw none of that softness in Orin's frame. He shivered at the image of where Orin could place those strong hands and move him exactly how he wanted. And surprisingly, he didn't fear being powerless with Orin. In fact, he hungered for it.

Taking a deep breath, he gathered his thoughts, noticing how they went around the crowds and those in line, straight to the doors and inside.

Gavin knew about the aquarium but had never been interested enough to pay the fee to go in. He worked, and whatever money he had, he kept. Fun money didn't exist when he was putting away just-in-case money. Tony paid him well, but Gavin was careful. His old habits of preparing for a necessary or hurried departure were embedded in his daily thought processes. A visit here was a luxury he felt he could do without, but he couldn't hide the thrum of excitement in his veins as they moved forward.

One of the attendants handed them a map, bowing to Orin. Orin smiled back, touching the man briefly on his shoulder, murmuring words Gavin didn't understand. Was it Spanish? No, it didn't sound like that.

Before Gavin could give it much thought, they moved on to the first room's entrance. He found himself mesmerized by the dancing jellyfish surrounding him. Then, in the center of the room was a tank taller than him, with an octopus sliding around the replica of a sunken ship.

Orin hummed gently, and as if in answer, the octopus rose,

leaving the ship and moving toward them. Pulling Gavin with him, Orin placed his hand against the glass. Gavin gaped in shock when the octopus reached out to Orin.

"Hello, my friend. I see they keep you fed well here. How does it feel to be a king, the center of attention?"

The octopus's color flushed, the almost bluish gray becoming a gentle red. He rocked, then spun his tenacles about.

"What's happening?" Gavin said. He wasn't familiar with sea life. He was a good swimmer, but the idea of being fish food wasn't on his top ten list. Still, this had to be weird, right? He knew octopuses were intelligent, one of the smartest creatures in the sea. He'd seen the TikTok videos. But Orin seemed to be having a conversation. And that shouldn't be possible.

"Offering my respect. Every life deserves to be seen and admired. To know they are precious." Orin smiled, running his fingers across the glass, the octopus following them with his tentacles. "Fair well."

Orin tugged Gavin gently, and they continued their journey.

Chapter Seven

Orin watched Gavin devour a bag of cotton candy, licking his fingers as he went. He'd noticed his mate didn't hold himself back from enjoying experiences and could tell this was Gavin's first time at the aquarium. Gavin smiled and laughed joyfully as they visited each animal, even if he didn't quite understand the communion Orin shared with what he considered family. Gavin simply seemed to be enjoying a new experience. Knowing he was sharing a taste of his world with his mate made the evening so much better. He would have to thank Tony for suggesting the aquarium.

Orin had kept an eye on Gavin, looking for signs of fear or distaste at seeing a part of Orin's life, though encapsulated in a building when the sea itself was vast. Instead, Gavin showed only admiration.

Orin was not as familiar with human children as some were, but he imagined Gavin's joy and curiosity would be comparable to a child's. Seeing him touch the stingrays, first with hesitation, then with respect and awe, filled Orin's heart with happiness.

When they arrived at the reef display, Gavin appeared stunned, and even Orin was impressed. The sponges and oysters layered with clams and crabs were vibrant and created a cohesiveness that rivaled a work of art. The corals in yellowish-oranges, blues, and brilliant purples contrasted with brown and red sea urchins.

"I've seen it on television, on those diving shows? But I've never been this close before. It's amazing."

Orin had to agree, but this human-maintained coral garden hardly compared to the treasure he cared for at home. The display needed some fish, more colors, and varieties. To watch his mate admire his garden, witnessing those magical grey eyes filled with wonder at the color and precious life he'd worked so diligently to cultivate, would be a dream realized.

"It is. Imagine seeing it all for yourself where it is meant to be appreciated?" Orin gave Gavin a gentle kiss, hungry for a taste of him. He wanted to show Gavin so much more. Who knew how much time he had before he needed to return?

And no, he would not be returning alone.

He led Gavin out of the building to walk along the waterfront. The moon hung high in the sky, her light dancing in dapples across the water's surface. If he listened closely, he could easily distinguish the sounds of his home, the chirps and hums of the sea, a musical piece that called to his soul.

Orin drew his mate close as they walked, enjoying his easy company.

"You ever wonder what it's like?" Gavin mused.

Orin searched his brain for what he might have missed. Neither had spoken in some time, content with gentle caresses and the beat of cresting waves.

"Wonder what what is like?"

Better to ask than dive into the unknown.

"To live in the ocean."

Orin nearly choked. "What do you mean, exactly?"

"Well, here we are in our world, existing, concerned with our own issues when right out there is a world many of us know nothing about." Gavin pointed out toward the darkness, gasping when a flicker of a tail moved above the surface. "Woah. Did you see that?"

"I saw something." And he had, choosing ignorance instead.

"Wonder what it was." Gavin tugged Orin closer to the water.

"Hm," Orin said. "I wonder." He couldn't say it was one of his Guardians, no doubt testing how close they could get without drawing too much attention, possibly Kasha or

Vashti. He wouldn't worry. If there were a concern, someone would have opened a circle to speak with him by now. He saw the glints of gold on a fin and knew it was Vashti who was being nosy.

Orin smiled and gently pulled Gavin to him, kissing him while shooing one of his best Guardians away. Pauric had probably done some talking. He was due for a warning.

Gavin sighed when Orin let him go, licking his lips hungrily.

"What was that for? Not that I'm complaining. I like your lips on mine." Gavin spoke in a whisper, soft and warm, inviting, but his gaze was off to the side as if afraid to admit what he wanted.

"I do as well. I look forward to many more moments such as these." Orin smiled when Gavin glanced at him searchingly, smiling. He pulled Gavin against him tightly, kissing him once again.

He took Gavin to a restaurant where someone could serve his mate instead. He'd witnessed Gavin working hard every moment in Tony's restaurant. His mate deserved to be treated as the prince he was.

They talked about their trip to the aquarium, Orin hanging on every word that fell from his mate's lips.

He enjoyed watching Gavin interact with others. Their server, a brown-haired, brown-skinned beauty, seemed enthralled, laughing at Gavin's witty statements about the food. Orin suddenly envisioned slicing the man's life short with a mere touch from his trident or snapping his windpipe with two fingers.

What is this? This feeling where he found it disturbing that Gavin's lovely smiles and gentle laughs weren't his alone. Very unlike him to feel such violence when he was typically calm and level-headed.

When the server leaned closer, his hand on Gavin's shoulder, Orin cleared his throat. The man turned Orin's way, eyes widening when Orin smiled. The smile he donned before battle—icy and cold, filled with sweet and bloody promise.

The server backed off—no more touches, no more being a flirty seahorse. Gavin looked at Orin, his lips curved into a careful yet pleased smile. He placed one of his hands over Orin's with a knowing twinkle in his eye. Orin found himself quite fond of that twinkle.

Orin easily imagined himself enjoying Gavin for years to come, working for the shy grins and the soft laugh, reveling in bliss as though he'd won a bounty.

Still, he wanted tears. Whimpers and cries. He longed for Gavin to bear his marks.

Gavin shyly looked up and then glanced away. "You're quiet, Orin."

"This is true. Lost in thoughts of you, of possibilities." Orin licked his lips, enjoying Gavin's barely noticeable gasp and hearing the faster pace of his mate's beating heart. "You fascinate me, and there is so much I want to see with you, to do with you. To you."

Gavin's gaze dropped to the table and back to Orin. "I'm no one special, especially for someone like you."

Orin leaned closer. "Someone like me?"

Gavin waved a hand in Orin's direction. "When I look at you, I see royalty, someone important. A warrior. I'm ordinary. I work in a restaurant. I go there and back home. I read books to live through characters who do my adventuring for me. You? I can tell there's more to you than just being one of Tony's relatives. You're a leader, someone who demands submission."

Orin noticed Gavin's breath quicken as he spoke. Whatever Gavin saw in Orin brought a lustful heat to his golden skin.

"I do lead, Gavin. And I demand submission."

Gavin shifted in his seat.

"Do you like that, Gavin? The idea of submitting? Do you like the idea of submitting to me?"

Gavin glanced up, his cheeks a deeper blush, a sure sign of his arousal. "It's been a while since I've allowed someone to have that kind of power over me."

Orin felt the tips of his canines grow sharp at the thought of Gavin's submission. He took a deep breath, centering himself. He had better control than this.

"Your submission would be a gift, my beautiful one. A gift I would treasure and never take for granted." He skated a finger over Gavin's palm. "I won't ask you to make such a decision on our first night together. For now, it's enough being here in your presence."

This time, Gavin licked his lips, and Orin's mind suddenly envisioned that tongue spearing his ass, delving deep within his body. He fell back against his chair, shocked at the image.

"Orin?" Gavin asked, worriedly moving to stand but remaining seated at Orin's indication.

What are these thoughts? His breaths were harsh, his hands shaking.

Orin looked at Gavin, his heart racing. "All is well. I believe we should go for a walk and enjoy some fresh air." Movement, action, that was what he needed. All of this was new to him. His immediate draw to Gavin. Barely considering his responsibilities below the surface. And now . . . sexual thoughts where he would find himself vulnerable?

Though he didn't find it an unwelcome thought.

Perhaps it *was* what he needed? It would bear some consideration.

For now, he took Gavin's hand in his, placed enough bills on the table to cover the price of the meal, and led his mate outside.

Chapter Eight

Gavin stood at his kitchen counter, stirring honey into his peppermint tea. He watched from the window as his neighbor's dogs chased each other, smiling when one slid in the wet grass. The black lab shook his head, recovered, and resumed the game while the other, also black and just as eager to play, skirted around the lab happily.

He'd been staring and stirring his tea for so long it had gone lukewarm. He sighed and gave up on the drink, pouring it into the sink, rinsing the cup, and placing it in the dish drainer. He shook his head, realizing his whole morning had been going the same way. He would start a task, and time would pass before he realized he had been wandering in a daze. He was useless, since his mind focused more on the previous night—the tender kisses and playful touches—than on what he needed to accomplish that day. The date had been an evening of Orin edging and teasing him with the possibility of more.

Submission. Orin wanted Gavin to submit to him, to offer control over his needs. It was a scary yet heady request.

Riordan had robbed him of the ability to let go without fear after too many trips to the hospital with knowing looks and cards offering support. Too many nights culminating in tears of frustration and the trauma of so many bruises, not the good kind.

Can I do it again? Can I take a chance?

He was probably being foolish, since he knew deep down it wasn't a matter of *if* but *when*.

If Orin had asked Gavin before leaving him at his door, he would have immediately knelt at the man's feet, head against the toe of his boot. Letting Orin kiss him deeply enough to feel when he awoke, but not having the entire experience? He

51

ached.

What had spooked Orin during dinner, though? That look of uncertainty? Was it fear? And then his strange need to leave the restaurant to get that fresh air he spoke of before practically pulling Gavin outside. It was sudden. Weird.

And driving him insane because he felt something reacting deep inside. Seeing the powerful man's vulnerability called to him with an urgency, both protective and thrilling.

Gavin's cell buzzed, snapping his attention back to the present, and he smiled when he saw the message.

So, how was it?

Of course Coralia wanted to know details. He could just keep her waiting, make her wonder.

Don't make me come over there. You know I will. In fact . . .

Gavin sighed when he heard knocking at his front door only seconds later. He went to the door, partially cracking it open to see his friend with a bag from one of their favorite bagel places that had better contain a cherry cream cheese Danish. How often did a person start the day with their favorite treat? Boiled eggs and tea could only get a person so far when sugar was the real motivating factor in this thing called life.

"Yes, I have what your sweet-tooth-loving self is craving here." She waved the bags teasingly. "Now, open the door and let me in, or I'll eat them both!"

"Nope!" Gavin reached out, snatching the bags and holding them close to his heart. He gave Coralia a sly smile before throwing the door open and waving her inside. "You can have whatever you want for these."

Coralia's laugh made Gavin smile as he led the way to the kitchen, licking the few crumbs he'd pinched from the Danish.

"Delicious!" Gavin set the bags down and poured two cups of coffee. "Coffee tastes so much better with a Danish."

"Only the best for the best." Coralia took the cup Gavin

offered and sat at the island, humming when she sipped, her gaze tracking Gavin's every move.

At times, Coralia moved like a predator, missing nothing. She would be dangerous if she weren't so loving. Or maybe she was more dangerous when she loved. Gavin mentally shrugged. As long as she was on his side, what did it matter?

Gavin sighed. Did having power remove a person's vulnerability or capacity to love? Orin was such a powerful and physically imposing man, draped in a deep brown sheath of flesh, and Gavin wanted to slip and slide his tongue all over. Orin was a leader from the core out. When he spoke, others listened, following his commands without question. There were commands Gavin longed to follow. All Orin had to do was ask.

"Earth to Gavin. What's that look about? Is that Danish getting some devotion that should probably go to a certain someone?"

Gavin snorted, popping the last of the treat in his mouth. Shrugging, he set two plates on the island, knowing Coralia wouldn't disappoint him with the contents of the second bag. He smiled as he pulled out two wrapped hot bagels filled with meat and cheese. After placing them on the plates, he slid one closer, then sat and dug in.

"Gavin? I'm waiting. And stuffing your face won't deter me. I'm rather tenacious."

She was, he had no doubt. How many times had he tried to evade her questions to no avail? When she'd finished interrogating him, he always learned more about himself. And when it got to be too much, she would give him the space he needed. Maybe today would be one of those moments.

Glancing Coralia's way, he smiled and then wiped his face. Sitting back, he crossed one leg over the other. "I want to fuck him." There. He'd said it. It was out there. Coralia's investigative skills not required.

"Okay, when you say you want to fuck him, are we talking about lackluster Bob or someone dark and fascinating?" Coralia took a bite of her breakfast bagel, eyes rolling back with pleasure.

"Good?"

"Orgasmic. Now, answer the question." Coralia smiled, waiting.

"Orin." Stated without hesitation, and Gavin wanted to pat himself on the back.

She nodded. "And by fuck him . . ."

"I want to slide my dick in his ass and claim him."

Whew! That felt good. Cathartic even.

This desire to claim and own was a new feeling for him. A boldness he'd only displayed as a dancer, a time when he freely expressed himself. But this driving need couldn't, wouldn't be contained. And now that he'd said it out loud, that was all he wanted.

"Well. Wow, Gavin. Is this new for you?" Coralia set down her sandwich, her focus entirely on Gavin.

"Yes, it is, and it's all I can think about. Something about Orin sets me on fire, like I've needed him all my life and having him is vital."

Coralia took a deep breath. "I see."

"Do you? Because I don't. I have no idea what's happening to the Gavin I know. This Gavin wants to do things and have things. Things I would never have considered before meeting Orin. Coralia, I promise you I'm not crazy." He frowned. "Or maybe I am." That could explain it all. Maybe somewhere along the way, after escaping the craziness of his ex-lover, moving to a new city where he restarted his life, and meeting a man who made him incredibly thirsty for whatever he could get, he had lost his mind.

Yes, that had to be it.

"No, I don't think you're crazy. No, don't shake your head like that, Gavin. People change. Sometimes literally." There seemed to be more Coralia wanted to say when a thoughtful look crossed her face.

"Literally?"

"Maybe now isn't the time for this discussion, or at least not with me. But what you're feeling? Try not to question yourself." Coralia took a deep breath, apparently struggling with what to say.

That worried Gavin, because his friend was a master with words who never lacked something to say. "Coralia?"

"Oh, Gavin, if I could tell you, I would, but this is for you and Orin to share, especially if what I suspect is happening is really happening. And if it is, you both have some decisions to make." His friend took a breath, crossing her arms while smiling at him with a dopey look.

"I'm even more confused."

"I know, and I'm not making it any better, and for that, I'm sorry. Once you and Orin have the talk you desperately need to have, I promise to be there for you. Now, other than wanting to get inside him — and it's killing me not to explore that further — what do you think about him?"

Gavin's mind spun in a full circle. Finding Coralia capable of keeping something from him threw him for a loop and only made him even more curious. His friend was not known for her ability to keep things close to her chest.

Does this frighten or encourage me?

When he thought about it, fear might be an option but not a deterrent. This new Gavin wanted to explore these desires, refusing to be thwarted by his past insecurities or the one relationship he used to set the bar. That bar had been incredibly low and should have been tossed out years ago. No more wallowing in the quicksand of his and Riordan's terrible relationship.

No, he wanted what he and Orin could become.

He stared directly into Coralia's eyes. "I think he's my future."

Gavin rushed to his car. He'd spent too much time telling Coralia how much Orin fascinated him on their date and how the man smiled when he talked about coral. The way Orin described coral as a dragon sharing its horde was endearing. The man practically glowed when he spoke about the reef, and seeing his happiness had made Gavin hard as fuck.

He wanted to spend time with Orin and learn more about him. He craved the wicked smile hiding secrets he could only imagine.

Gavin easily pictured himself being tied up at Orin's mercy one moment and Orin on the end of his cock the next. No limitations. He wanted it all.

Shaking his head, he threw everything in the car, pressing the ignition button. As he pulled the gear shift into reverse, he looked up to see a note attached to his windshield. The paper appeared to be torn from a spiral notebook, and dark lettering could be seen scrawled on the page.

Gavin put the car in park and glanced around. Nothing appeared out of the ordinary. One of his neighbors was walking his dog, or rather, the dog walked him. Gavin smiled, laughing aloud at how the Cane Corso wrapped himself around his daddy's legs. Turning back to the note, he dropped his phone in the passenger seat, opened the door, and reached around to grab the paper.

When he opened the folded note, a white feather fell from within, carried by a light wind before settling on the ground at his feet. Confused, he picked up the feather, sliding his fingers over the barbs before fully opening the sheet to read its contents.

Hope is the thing with feathers — Emily Dickinson

A poem? What did that even mean?

Reading further, he saw one word.

Forgive.

The handwriting was more of a scribble, but he didn't

recognize it. He glanced from the feather to the note when his third alarm went off, which reminded him he should be well on his way to work. He tossed both items on the passenger seat, slid into the driver's seat, and took off.

Gavin was so focused on who might be following him that making it to work had been completely on autopilot.

Later, as he started his shift at the restaurant, the words from the note returned to the forefront of his mind. Had someone mistaken his car for someone else's? Was it from someone's romantic boyfriend or girlfriend apologizing for cheating?

But what if . . .

No. He was safe. He had a new life now.

Besides, in what world would Riordan have ever apologized for the terror he made of Gavin's old life? Riordan was an entitled ass who enjoyed using his parents' power to menace others.

Those words? Riordan would never.

No, there would be threats and poisoned promises.

Gavin shivered in fear. How many times had he looked behind himself on the way to work? And the feeling of being followed when he arrived? Was it just his imagination, or was the note truly meant for him? A threat? A plea?

Gavin just wanted to continue his life, safe from abuse and surrounded by friends. Now, he was checking dark corners, hyperaware of anything and anyone that wasn't part of his current normal.

He hated feeling his old fears gathering around his heart like a butterfly's pupa, a cocoon he'd escaped years ago.

Would he continue to spread his wings and fly, or allow fear to tear the appendages from his back, slamming him to the ground?

He looked around the restaurant. He had friends here. Coralia, Jenny, Tony . . . Tony was more like an older brother than a boss. He could confide in almost anyone here, but even years later, he still didn't trust it. Friendship hadn't helped him in the past. The few friends he'd had back then deserted him, but he couldn't blame them. Riordan made being a friend dangerous with threats and innuendos.

Could he trust a friend now? Tell someone he thought he was being followed, that his past had finally caught up with him, and he didn't know what to do?

After he'd escaped, he had never looked back. And now what? Had Riordan tracked him down somehow and now left poetry on his car?

No.

Gavin wasn't giving up the happiness he'd found. Not his friends, his job, his home, and especially not the man he was coming to think of as his own.

Hope is the thing with feathers . . .

Okay, well, he wasn't letting his hope fly away.

Once again, Orin sat at the bar of Iliona's Safe Haven as he watched Gavin work. His mate had a tightness to his movements that hadn't been there before, his usual fluidity missing as he traversed the restaurant from table to table.

Orin had debated coming to the restaurant, nervous about how Gavin made him feel. He wanted to give this man things he'd never shared with another. Falling asleep the evening before had proven difficult with thoughts of how it would feel to have his mate inside him, taking him.

Yet his confusion hadn't kept him away.

No, he'd come, his cheeks wearing an indentation into the bar stool that had become his domain as he hungrily watched his mate. Because he wanted, craved, and was very nearly ready to beg Gavin to take him tonight. He shifted in his seat, doing his best to hide the need visible to all who chanced a look between his thighs.

Yet as he watched his mate, the way Gavin's eyes darted toward the door, canvasing the area, his carnal needs took a step back, his need to protect what was his quickly moving to the forefront.

Tony stood at the bar while helping the youngest of his brood with his studies, clicking until he'd found a video they could use as an example before turning to Orin. "What will it be?"

"Come now, Tony, you know my favorite by now."

Tony laughed. "Root beer float on its way, fine sir."

The delectable treat had become an addiction for Orin, one he could see himself returning to the shore to enjoy in the future. Gavin had laughed at the novelty of Orin enjoying such a treasure. Gavin's easy smile and the husky laugh he'd shared had made him hard as a rock. Who needed a delicious root beer float when Gavin was the option?

He pulled himself back to the present. "Thank you, Tony. Have you noticed anything different about him today?" He angled his chin, indicating Gavin.

Tony pulled a container of ice cream from the fridge beneath the bar, along with a container of cinnamon. He glanced over to Gavin and back. "Other than being quieter than usual? Not really. The girls tried talking to him, but his focus was on work. As his boss, I can't say having someone focused on their job is bad. As his friend, maybe it's a little worrisome. We like the Gavin he's become."

"The one he's become?" Orin remembered Coralia's tales of a problematic life his mate had experienced. There would be no more of that for Gavin. He would be treasured and loved, protected always. The only pain he would undergo would be pleasure at Orin's hands.

"Yes. From what I gather, there was a boyfriend who kept him like a prisoner and an asshole family that used their money to ensure he stayed that way. When he first arrived, he was always looking over his shoulder, searching the shadows." Tony poured the root beer before dropping a scoop of ice cream in and sprinkling it with the cinnamon. He snorted at Orin's raised brow and added a small hill of whipped cream with a cherry on the top.

"Do we have a name for this man? Know what happened to him?" Orin sucked deeply through the straw before popping the cherry into his mouth. He thought back to the other evening when he'd sensed an unknown danger. Unfortunately, Pauric had been unable to discover anything, returning to the restaurant empty-handed. They'd kept watch, though.

"Jordan? Aiden?" Tony shrugged. "I'm not sure. He doesn't bring him up. I think I've only heard the name once."

Orin nodded, sucking more of the liquid down, enjoying

the sugar rush flowing through his system. These were probably bad for his health. No matter. He would return home someday, and these would no longer be an option.

"He is different tonight. I learn more about him as we spend more time together. This pensive, watchful Gavin is new." Orin sipped his drink.

"Not to us." Tony glanced at Gavin and then back. "This is the one we met."

"Unacceptable. I need to know why."

"I have to tell you." Tony leaned on the bar. "I love seeing how Gavin acts around you."

Orin sucked the last bit down. "I do as well."

"All right then. How about I let him off early tonight? You can take him home and see if you're able to get him to open up." Tony answered a question for his youngest, then moved to the following video.

Orin looked around. The restaurant was packed with diners enjoying conversation and food. He wasn't a restauranteur, but he wondered about the staff if he took Gavin with him. "And you'll be adequately supported tonight?"

"Yes, we'll be adequately supported." Tony laughed. "I wouldn't put myself out, and I'd like to know Gavin's taken care of, that his mind is at ease. He's a good kid, almost like a little brother. And I believe you're just as good for him as he is for you."

"Thank you. I am honored." Orin was confident of his place beneath the surface, knew his purpose, and had known it all his life. He was born to be a Guardian, blessed with the gift perhaps before his mother gave birth to him. But to be given such trust here? It was a gift he would not squander.

Tony smiled and then nodded toward Gavin. "Give me a moment to talk to him, then I'll send him to you. He's not one to typically think about leaving early. He works doubly hard to impress the rest of us. After all this time, I feel he's still not sure he can step back and realize he's earned his place."

Orin nodded. Trust was hard won. No one wished to fail, to lose their place or their home. In his struggles, Gavin had found his sanctuary. The thought of losing such a place would worry him, Orin was sure.

He waited as Tony moved from behind the bar. He refused to be embarrassed as he slurped the rest of his drink from the glass, even licking the sugary rim before setting the glass on the counter.

He smiled warmly when his mate arrived at his elbow.

Gavin glared, his arms crossed, hands grasping his elbows tightly. "So, I'm off early, still getting paid, and have been told . . . No, I've been commanded to go home with you." He had a bite in his tone that Orin was not accustomed to but discovered he liked.

Orin turned to fully face Gavin, searching the countenance he'd come to admire greatly. "Yes, it would appear so. You don't wish to spend time with me?"

Gavin would do him well as a mate, tall and beautiful, with a kindness he'd displayed many times in his interactions with others. But this spirit, this anger, was something new. It called to Orin like a siren, challenging the fire in his spirit.

He leaned closer to the man who had captured him the moment he first saw him. "Are you afraid of me, Gavin?"

Gavin's eyes sparkled. "Should I be?"

"There are times, yes, when you should fear me. Fear the blaze burning within me for you, the way I would decimate any fool stupid enough to touch what is mine." He leaned forward, sliding his chin along Gavin's cheek, savoring the softness of his mate's skin as he whispered, "Make no mistake, Gavin. You are mine."

Gavin trembled, and Orin felt the vibration to the depths of his soul. As he'd hoped, his words settled Gavin, his shoulders dropped, his tension becoming a whisper rather than an active volcano. Gavin sighed, then leaned the rest of the way into Orin's arms, laying his head on Orin's chest. Orin kissed him gently on his temple before taking a moment to swipe his tongue across his skin. He breathed in the scent of his mate, barely catching his fangs before they dropped.

Not now. This is not the place.

He whispered into Gavin's ear. "There you are, my sweet. Let me take you home. Allow me to keep you safe. Allow me to care for you."

"This is hard."

Orin didn't doubt that, but he wanted to prove to this man, who had given a small part of himself, that he could take and treasure all of him. "Please allow me to try."

Chapter Ten

Orin took Gavin's hand and headed into his temporary residence, a sanctuary built by Kamau for his return trips to the surface to fulfill his mate Graham's need to visit family. Kamau had built the two-storied home with multiple bedrooms, a library, a kitchen, a study, and plenty of space. He shared the shelter with family or friends who wished to visit the surface in comfort while exploring a world sometimes unkind to those from the sea or different from what society perceived acceptable.

When he'd first arrived on the land at Pauric's bidding, he'd thought the adventure would be a waste of time for him. He'd imagined spending his time longing for his coral garden and the comfort of the home he knew. Never did he believe he would find his future. Sure, he'd done some hopeful wishing . . . praying . . . since his brothers had discovered their mates here.

Kamau had lived much of his early life on the surface, half-mer half-human, a siren abused by his father. His human father had been a despicable blur on the human race, unworthy of their mother's love, but it had not destroyed Kamau. Any relationship with his sire became discarded dreams when the man tried to murder Graham, his son's mate. Instead, with the help of his mate, Kamau had found himself and realized his strengths to thwart his father's plans. Then he'd taken Graham to his home beneath the waves, where he would be treasured throughout his lifetime.

And then there was Batair. He'd felt the pull of his mate while far beneath the surface, deep within Atlantis. He'd climbed between the roll of the waves, determined to claim his future. Yes, he had to wear down his dragon mate, Aoki. But it wasn't long before Batair became a father and a valued treasure to his Aoki. Orin visited them through the circle, the portal used by the mer to communicate with each other over great distances.

Of course, Trillian had also found his mate on land. Who could have known he would find the long-lost Guardian, Tetra Lindh, who had deserted their world? But none could have blamed Lindh when his first mate—mother to his children, Coralia and Adamaris—was brutally murdered by a fellow Guardian. Trillian and Lindh now lived beneath the surface, an artist and his masterpiece.

The fire his brothers and their mates experienced had not died but only blazed greater beyond adversity. If they could attain their dreams, why not him?

Orin glanced worriedly at the man he desired above all else. Gavin had been alarmingly silent since they'd left the restaurant. He didn't know if Gavin could even fathom what they could possibly mean to each other. Orin had certainly felt it from the moment he saw Gavin.

He is mine.

He gently wrapped his hand around Gavin's wrist, drawing him forward, his heart melting when Gavin's gray eyes looked at him. Yet he sensed his mate's tension, his eyes a shallow reflection of their former beauty.

Where was his Gavin? Was he buried beneath layers of fear, working diligently to protect himself?

"I have an idea." He needed to help his mate feel safe. Even his skin was cold and clammy to the touch. "Do you trust me, Gavin?"

"I want to. I think I do, but I'm having a hard time trusting myself right now."

Orin smiled, kissing Gavin softly. "Come with me."

Orin looked his fill at the exquisite creature kneeling before him as he sat in a chair he'd pulled from the corner of the largest bedroom. He'd claimed this room for himself the moment he arrived. He was a sizeable man who required space and was glad the room could accommodate what he needed to do to help his mate.

He spent a moment admiring his mate's beautiful body. The chilled air was obviously not the only reason Gavin's nipples pebbled. His naked skin revealed a blush all over that Orin craved to sample with his tongue.

Gavin knelt silently on the hardwood floor, head bent and trembling slightly.

Orin leaned forward, breathing in Gavin's scent. "I could become addicted to you, Gavin, to the power you have over my senses."

Gavin glanced up and quickly away. "I'm not powerful." His voice was barely a whisper.

Orin heard every word and smiled. "My sweet, fierce darling. You have more power in the smallest digit of your graceful foot than most are foolish to believe they hold in their fist."

Orin shifted the silken ropes between his fingers as he stood. He looped the first of many around Gavin's shoulders, taking care to make them tight, securing his mate's arms to his side.

Gavin's sigh was unexpected but welcome as he gently rocked into Orin's touch like a dance as Orin wrapped him in layer after layer. He touched and kissed, gentling him.

As Orin worked, he touched, kissed, soothed, gentling Gavin and humming his approval as Gavin gifted him with his trust.

His submission.

When he finished, Gavin remained quiet, his eyes glazed, his body swaying almost imperceptibly.

"How do you feel, my beautiful sea anemone?" Orin placed a hand beneath Gavin's chin, lifting until he saw the muscles straining in Gavin's throat.

Gavin moaned.

"Words, mate." Orin rubbed his thumb against Gavin's full lips before dipping it inside the wet heat.

"I don't know what to say. I feel good, better than good." Gavin slid his tongue up the length of Orin's thumb, suckling.

Orin shivered, doing his best to maintain control. Gavin needed him to be steady, not succumbing to the delicious temptation of his mouth.

"Are you uncomfortable?"

Gavin moaned. "No, I feel safe. I feel like I can breathe. It was hard to breathe." His words sounded drugged, his eyelids fluttering.

"Good. Ropes can help. Ironically, being trapped within bindings can be freeing." Orin removed his finger, bending down to kiss Gavin's lips. "I will lift you now and place you on the bed."

Gavin nodded.

Orin smiled, gently picked up his mate, and carried him to the bed. He sat next to him, sliding his hands over and between the ropes, savoring the sighs and moans.

Gavin tried to lean into Orin's touch, but with the ropes tied about his frame, there was little he could do but accept Orin's touches. He sighed. "I had a boyfriend, a guy I was seeing."

The words were soft, and Orin nodded, continuing to touch and kiss, his strokes a gentle praise.

"In the beginning, I was impressed with him, the things he would do and buy for me. He gave me gifts and took me on trips."

Orin slid his fingers into Gavin's hair, running the fingertips over his scalp.

"But it was a trap. He pretended to be in love with me, and I was blind to the monster he was." Gavin trembled.

Orin pulled on a rope, tightening it. In response, Gavin

calmed and accepted a kiss against his lips.

"The first time he hit me, I had come home late, and somehow Riordan—that was . . . is his name . . . Riordan was sitting in a chair inside my apartment. At that time, I hadn't given him a key. It should have been a warning sign, a red flag. Maybe some part of me knew that Riordan having a key was a bad idea, but it didn't seem to matter. He was there, and he was angry. He thought I was with someone, not remembering I worked late, practicing. He had gone by the studio and didn't see me. I'd gone out to get something to eat and decided to eat there. I had forgotten to charge my phone, so I didn't call. Meanwhile, he worked himself up into a rage."

Gavin paused then, and Orin caressed his neck, keeping him tethered to the present.

"I had to take a few days off work. It was hard to walk, hard to sit. I knew then I needed to get away from him, somehow. Riordan paid the director to fire me and threatened the other dancers who tried to help me find work. He broke my lease. I had nowhere to go. When I moved in with the few friends I had left, their lives became terrible. I ended up back with him.

"I lived with him, was kept dependent on him with no one to help. His parents believed Riordan needed me, so they used their money to keep me trapped. Until one day the cleaning lady they'd hired decided she'd had enough of me being a broken doll. She helped free me. Gave me a place to run to, and I came here. And for so long, I've been safe."

Gavin paused, breathing deeply. "But today, there was a note on my car. A message. And shit . . . I'm scared, Orin, so fucking scared that Riordan's found me." Tears flowed down his cheeks.

Orin bent to kiss them away. "I've got you, Gavin. Tell me about the note." He wrapped his arms around Gavin, lying against him and holding him tight.

Orin listened as Gavin told him about the note, committing the details to his memory. *Hope?* Had the person left the message as a threat, or was it a plea for forgiveness?

"Was there anything else other than the feather?"

"No." His mate sounded tired, clearly drained — the ropes, the release, all of it coming to a head.

Tenderly, Orin removed the ropes, unwinding Gavin's body, rubbing his arms and legs, his waist, and shoulders until he was warm. Then he pulled the blanket lying at the foot of the bed and covered them both.

"I thought we were going to —"

"No." Orin placed a finger over Gavin's lips. "Maybe tomorrow, but right now, my love, I only wish to hold you."

Gavin was asleep a moment later, his chest slowly rising and falling, safe in the circle of Orin's arms.

Chapter Eleven

Gavin's eyes fluttered open. He flexed his arms and felt the absence of the ropes that had bound his soul, freeing him as Orin had said they would. He vaguely remembered Orin removing them. He'd been in a daze, revealing truths he'd promised never to speak to anyone.

But the note, the fear of being imprisoned again, had wrapped him in the nightmare of his past. He'd been oblivious to people at work, lost in a time he should have shed long ago.

Gavin wanted to be angry at Tony's suggestion of going home with Orin, so he'd spit venom at the man he dreamed of being next to.

Yet Orin had made him feel safe. Loved. Protected. He'd needed Orin, needed the restraint.

The binding had been a gift.

"Awake, Gavin?"

Gavin turned to look at the man beside him, amazed they lay together. He'd craved this, their closeness, among other things.

"Yes."

"Tell me again."

He frowned. "Tell you what?"

Orin rose onto his elbow, sliding his other hand along Gavin's thigh. His nails turned sharp, piercing skin as they went. "Last night, you said you believed we would mate."

Gavin moaned when fingers, wet with what was probably his blood, wrapped around his cock, stroking slowly. "Fuck."

"It's what I've wanted for some time now." Orin moved over him, sliding his larger body over Gavin's. Placing his hands on both sides of Gavin's head, he kissed him, biting at his lips and pushing against him.

Gavin's body went into sensory overload, his hands reaching to touch Orin everywhere, moaning into the kiss that was sucking all of his air. Orin became his oxygen, his lifeblood.

When Orin lifted his head, his features were different, like some creature Gavin had never seen. He remembered things he'd heard at the restaurant, stories from others about Tony's family. Whispers. But his body was too horny, too needy, to deal with it. No, he wanted to take and be taken.

Eyes that weren't human fixated on him, trapping him in their gaze.

Orin opened his mouth, showing teeth sharper than before. "Say yes."

Gavin could have questioned. He could have pushed Orin away and run. But he was tired of running, tired of questioning himself. This man, whatever the fuck Orin was, made him feel what no one else ever had. Gavin wouldn't give this up. He'd read books about mysterious creatures and enjoyed the paranormal. This could be a dream or his reality.

He wanted both, but he had to know. "What are you?"

"Merman. Guardian of the sea. Grandson to Neptune. Your mate. Say yes to me," Orin murmured. "I have ached all night lying beside you, burned with the thought of feeling you wrapped around my cock, spilling my seed into your body. Say yes to me."

"And if I said no?"

"I would work that much harder for the answer to be yes."

Gavin gasped when claws slid down his side, chest to hip, grasping at him tightly.

"Orin!"

"Say yes to me, Gavin."

Orin's eyes glowed as he rocked into Gavin, torturing him with his hard length. "Say yes to me. For me."

Gavin shouted out when he was suddenly flipped onto his

stomach, his legs stretched wide open, and Orin's face buried between his cheeks. Crying with tears falling over his face, he mewed, and now he was the one begging. "Please. Please, Orin."

Orin growled. "Your taste is divine. I would devour you daily. Allow you to be my nourishment. I would give you the world, the sea, and everything in between. Say yes to me, Gavin."

"Fuck. Fuck. Shit. Yes, Orin. Anything."

"Say you are mine, Gavin."

"I am yours!" Gavin screamed the words, pushed beyond his ability to control his need.

Orin covered him then, wide cock head at his hole, teeth at his throat, shoving forward.

Gavin tried to move, impaled on the rigid length, trapped. He could hear and feel Orin drinking from him as he took him, his thrusts rough, sinking into him, making the two of them one.

Tears slid down his cheeks, his lungs on fire from screaming.

"So beautiful in your pain, so completely mine," Orin murmured against his ear. "You are a treat, an ambrosia for the gods. You are mine, Gavin, and I would destroy anyone who would seek to take you from me. I will protect you until my breath is the very last." His words were punctuated with thrusts into Gavin's body, using his knee to spread him further, trying to get his entire body within Gavin's own.

Gavin whimpered, his body slamming against the bed, his dick sliding up the sheets before Orin wrapped his fist around his leaking length, tugging his orgasm out of his soul.

Orin latched onto Gavin's throat again, drinking deeply before licking and tucking Gavin closer. "I'm going to come inside you, gift you with my seed. It is a joy I have prayed for many years—for my mate to carry my inner being. You are a gift to me, Gavin, my treasure. Feel me, love all that will become of us. Accept me."

Gavin moaned, his body and soul wholly submitted to Orin. He trembled and shook, sobbing with pleasure as he was held tight against Orin's body. He felt loved. Treasured. Captured. Baptized in the needs of his lover. He didn't have to do anything but accept. Moaning that acceptance, he cried out when Orin's hot seed drenched his insides, searing as loop after loop coated his pulsing walls.

Orin licked at his skin, smiling against his swollen neck, those blades revisiting, teasing his flesh.

"You are my gift. I've lived a lifetime to have you, and now, you will have me forever." A final thrust inside, and Gavin collapsed, blackness enveloping him as Orin gently rocked within.

Moments passed, or was it days? He awoke to Orin touching him, caressing his skin, gently cupping his belly.

"There you are, my love. My mate. How do you feel?"

Gavin stretched, loving the feeling of Orin wrapped around him. "Coralia told me there was something you needed to tell me."

Merman. That's what Orin had said. Gavin remembered altered features, the feel of sharp teeth. He remembered Orin drinking from him, filling him with need instead of fear. His and Coralia's discussion came to mind, how he longed to do things to Orin, things that were unlike him.

"Ah, she would know."

"And it was that you are a merman?"

"Indeed, as is she. As is her brother, Tony's husband Adamaris. We are all family. All Neptune's blood. And now, you. You are also of Neptune, mate of mine."

"What does that mean?" How was he even accepting this conversation? Was it being bitten, sharing his blood, Orin's seed still coating him from the inside? Was it knowing this man, feeling safe with him last night? Was it having lived a nightmare, and no matter what happened now, nothing could be worse than nearly dying at the hands of someone completely human who was supposed to love him?

"It means you said yes to me, and I have claimed you." Orin turned Gavin into his arms. "It means you are mine to protect and love."

Gavin smiled, resting his head against Orin's shoulder. This was enough. It could be enough, but still. He wanted more. He'd told Coralia what he needed, but could he tell Orin and let him know that energy crawled around in his body and needed to be released into this man? How did that work when you loved a merman, a Guardian? He needed to know more about that, too.

"I need to know more about this part of you, Orin. Who and what you are and what a Guardian is."

"Yes, let's have this conversation somewhere I can focus on speaking with you. Being next to you like this doesn't help."

Chapter Twelve

Orin sat across the kitchen table from his mate. The distance would help, allowing him to concentrate as he explained their new life together.

His mate's acceptance of them was a part of the mate bond, but no one should go into life blind. There were facts Gavin must know if they were to survive. He drank a glass of root beer and glanced at Gavin's belly, wondering if he had planted his young successfully. He didn't hear a call.

"Orin?"

Refocusing, he tried to remember Gavin's question. "Yes, as a Guardian, I am a part of Neptune's army. I am a leader, with men and women to care for who even now wonder when I will return."

"Return?"

"Yes, to home. Our home, where we will have a family."

Gavin's eyes widened at that. "Family?"

Orin nodded, no longer able to endure even the table between them. He knelt at Gavin's feet, his head against his belly. "My hope is that within your body, my life begins. And yet, I hear nor feel anything. I thought I had surely impregnated you."

"Wait. What the fuck?" Gavin jumped up and pushed Orin away. "Impregnated me?"

Orin raised his hands, fingers spread in a hopefully calming way to his mate. "Yes, you said yes."

"Oh. Orin, you can't be serious." Gavin looked down at his body and up again, placing his hand over his stomach protectively. "You can't just breed someone. You have to explain. You can't assume I knew what saying yes means."

"You are mine. You said yes to us, to our future."

"To you, yes? To being pregnant? I'm just now grasping

the concept of being a merman's mate, and you throw possible daddy into the mix like I will give birth. That is not good, Orin. Who told you that was okay?"

Orin moved forward, but Gavin stepped back.

"No. No, not now." Gavin held up a hand. "Not right now. I love you. Yes, I can't believe what the hell is happening and how fucking fast this is, but I love you and your stupid dick and the way you make me feel, but being a father? What man has babies?"

"Gavin, Adamaris gave birth to his and Tony's baby. I'm pretty certain Tony's ready again. My brothers' children? All natural births to men. When you have our young, we will care for them as they have."

"Whoa." Gavin took a deep breath. "No. I'm not ready for this conversation."

Gavin still held his belly protectively, which delighted Orin, even though his mate looked as if he could stab him at that very moment. Though he felt nothing, no call from Gavin's body or sign of a child, he still hoped. Not wishing to agitate his mate, he moved back a step.

"I need to leave, okay? I'm going home," Gavin muttered. "I'm going to call an Uber to take me home. I need a few days to deal with this."

"No."

"No?"

"No, you will not have a few days. You are mine. You said yes to me." Fear began to spread throughout his body. "You are mine to protect. You would leave me?"

This time, it was Gavin who moved closer. "Quiet, Orin. My love, I need time." He placed a hand against Orin's cheek. "I need a day, maybe two. I need a little time to digest this because this is a lot. And I need you to understand."

Orin sighed, his hands drawing into fists, but he nodded. "Yes, my mate. Time you need, and time you will have."

"Thank you."

Hours passed, days it seemed, but Orin refused to leave his home, too afraid he would immediately find his mate and drag him back. When the third morning came, he found himself facing Pauric and Coralia at his door.

"You have sulked enough, Orin, don't you think?" Pauric crossed his arms while Coralia peeked around the corner.

"I am not sulking."

"Interesting. You are unbathed and less than your meticulous self." Pauric moved into the home then. "And I see no food about. Yes, sulking."

Coralia looked about. "You're not the only one."

Orin perked up at that. "Gavin?"

Coralia smiled. "Yes, he is equally as miserable."

Orin's heartbeat stuttered. "He asked me for time."

Coralia jabbed a finger at Orin's chest. "Yes, and you gave him that. Now, one of you must get your shit together, and since you're the one that scared the hell out of him, I choose you."

"He doesn't want my young." Orin heard the break in his voice as he spoke of the rejection.

Pauric sighed. "Orin, my friend. It is my understanding that Gavin has accepted our existence. That in itself is a feat. What frightened him was the realization he could give birth. That would surprise any human male." He stepped forward. "And I sensed nothing within him when we spoke, Orin."

"I thought . . ."

"No. There is nothing there. Just fear and tension, and above all else, heartbreak."

Orin's heart broke at his friend's words. "Then perhaps this was not meant and a waste for both of us. This time, I need time. Please."

"Orin?" Pauric reached out.

"No. I need time. Something must be wrong with me, and I must determine what to do next."

When Pauric and Coralia left, Orin retreated to his bed. Perhaps it was time to return to his home. Maybe he'd been here long enough. Maybe his mind was clouded, and time away from his people, his coral garden, had overwhelmed him. Was he seeing possibilities where none existed?

But he couldn't ignore the need humming through him whenever he thought of Gavin, of how he ached for him. He needed him desperately, so much that he dreamed of him, of Gavin touching him, filling him, mating him.

On the fourth day, he felt as if he were ill, his body turning hot and cold, his blood thrumming in his veins. He could no longer eat or drink. Perhaps he was dying. And wouldn't that be apt? His heart was gone, and his spirit, too.

He thought about the ocean, returning to the sea. It was obvious that Pauric would not be leaving, that he'd chosen his life here. Maybe it was time for Orin to go home.

Chapter Thirteen

Riordan paced back and forth. A note, that's what he had left, along with the feather. He remembered when Gavin enjoyed things like that, romantic gestures before Riordan had beat it out of him.

There was so much to apologize for, so much to be forgiven.

His new therapist had helped him with that, helped him realize that his fear of not being loved had worked to create the monster he'd become.

Abuse did that to a person.

But he wasn't that person anymore. Gradually, he'd found parts of his soul, the bits whittled away by his parents.

How could his mother have allowed him to be hurt? Why? Wasn't he worth more than the bastard she'd married?

Apparently not, but he was safe now.

Now, he watched Gavin, not sure of what to say or how to apologize for all he'd done.

How does a person apologize for becoming a monster? For almost killing someone they were supposed to love. His stepfather never had.

The guy usually with Gavin hadn't been there in days, and it looked like Gavin was suffering for it. Dark circles enhanced those gray eyes Riordan once thought he loved. Had he ever truly loved Gavin, or had Gavin always been someone to possess and vent his rage upon?

Had Riordan even been capable of love back then?

Riordan dropped money on the table. He'd been here multiple times, but Gavin had never waited on him. He'd hoped one day, but as if Gavin was wary of the darkness haunting him, someone else was always sent to his table.

Riordan probably looked different. Years of therapy after

nearly dying from a self-inflicted gun wound would do that to a person. He'd needed time to heal, both physically and mentally. During that time, he'd learned how much he hated himself and how much fear he carried. He'd also learned how to work on loving himself.

Part of that was reconciling his actions. He could have written a letter to Gavin. It hadn't taken long to find him once he'd gotten his shit together. Their maid being the one to beat the shit out of him had helped start his catharsis. He'd been an evil bastard.

He'd needed this change.

He was better, not good, not even great, but better.

Riordan waited outside next to his car, a simple Lexus sedan, unlike the sports cars he used to drive when looking for attention.

He saw Gavin exit the building and get into his vehicle, and then he followed him at a distance. He already knew where he lived after watching him for days now. Gavin was typically off on Sunday, working the rest of the week.

This could be my moment. Am I ready to face my demons?

When Gavin pulled into the parking space of his home, Riordan quickly jumped out of his car and ran to him.

"Gavin!"

Gavin turned to him, fear immediately filling his face. He stepped back, ready to throw what looked like a bag of food at him. "Fucking knew it. You can't have me. I have friends here . . . family. I have a mate. You can't take me back." He sounded terrified.

Riordan knew immediately he needed to calm Gavin and do his best to save what could be a terrible situation. "No, Gavin. No, please. I'm sorry. I've been trying to say that for days. I'm sorry." Riordan put a hand up and stepped forward.

"No, you stay there. You always say you're sorry, then you hurt me. I won't let you hurt me. You'll break his heart. He could die without me."

Gavin reached into his bag and pulled out a gun. His hand was steady, and Riordan realized this might be how he would be absolved. Dropping his hands, he closed his eyes and waited to be killed.

Chapter Fourteen

Orin was almost there. He'd debated with himself, wondering if he was making the right decision, but he couldn't just give up on them. Even if he failed his mate, he had to try one more time before he left to return home.

He missed Gavin. He felt himself deteriorating, shattering apart like broken glass.

And why? Because he was too stubborn to accept that he wasn't perfect, he was unable to impregnate his mate.

A bond was more than that. They didn't need to have young to have a life together. Surely he had enough in his family he could love.

He needed Gavin. It was time for him to fight.

He did not expect to arrive at his mate's home to see him wielding a weapon, aiming it at a young man standing in front of him. He had what appeared to be seconds before Gavin fired.

He called his mate's name, "Gavin!"

When Gavin turned to him, his eyes were trapped in the past, his body rigid with fear. He seemed to realize it was Orin and smiled before turning back to the man before him. "I'm going to kill him."

"Wait. Wait, my love. Are you certain? If you take this man's life, will it not erase your own?" Orin knew what it was to take a life, to feel the responsibility of ending another's existence. To never forget. He didn't want that for his mate.

"He's here to take me away from you. I can't leave you. I won't. I love you."

They were the words Orin needed to hear, but not in the circumstances he had dreamed of.

"I am so grateful, Gavin. I love you. More than life itself. But if he is to die, allow me to kill him so you may not have your life ruined by such a task. I will eviscerate him for you. Let me do this for you."

"No, I can do it."

The man in question looked like he'd accepted the outcome no matter the means.

"Who are you?" Orin asked.

The man turned to him. "My name is Riordan. I was Gavin's ex-boyfriend and a complete asshole to him. My therapist said a part of my healing was to apologize, but if I need to die, I can accept that, too."

"Apologize!" Gavin screamed. "You made my life a nightmare. You kept me a prisoner for so long that I forgot what it was to be free. You crippled every relationship I tried to have. I hate you."

Sorrowful eyes turned back to Gavin. "You have every right to hate me, Gavin. I hated myself, and I just didn't know how much. I'm sorry, so fucking sorry. I'm not asking to be with you, to come between you and the giant. I just wanted you to know that I know how awful I was and to let you know it wasn't your fault."

"Oh, I know that. It took me years to figure that out, but I know now. Who you were and what you did to me wasn't my fault. It never was."

Riordan nodded. "Hope is the thing with feathers. My hope is that my words would set you free."

Gavin lowered the gun. "Loving myself first and then allowing myself to be loved — that's what set me free."

Orin went to Gavin, wrapping him in his arms and removing the weapon. He kissed Gavin's eyelids, kissed the tears on his cheeks, and held him close.

Once Gavin was settled, he guided his mate back into his home and shut the door.

Then he turned to Riordan. "My mate may have forgiven you, but you are owed a reminder of why it is in your best interest to never pass this way again. Prove to me why that should not occur right now by my very hands."

The eyes that looked at him were wet with tears but absent of fear, showing only acceptance. "I don't know that I have a reason you'll accept. I failed him. Failed myself. He was in a living nightmare of my own making. I will say that I lived a nightmare of my own, but that's an excuse, not a reason to hurt him the way I did."

"You'll receive no absolution for your guilt here. It may never come. I won't kill you now, but I promise should we ever see you again, you will not have an easy death."

Riordan nodded. "I understand. He'll never see me again. I've done what I needed to do. Take care of him."

"Of that, you may never have a doubt."

Orin watched as the embodiment of his mate's nightmares got in his car and drove away. If he had not come, hoping desperately to gain his mate's love, something unforgivable could have happened. He turned back to the door when the lights from the car disappeared.

Inside, he found his mate pacing, the bags he'd carried on the floor beside the gun. He picked up the weapon, switched on the safety, and set it aside.

When he turned around, he found his arms full of a mate who was kissing him everywhere, nibbling at his neck, running his hands over his skin, tearing at his clothes.

"My love, my mate." Orin tried to hold him, tried to stop him. He was clearly in shock. He would not take him like this.

"Need you. Want you. I'm so cold. Will you keep me warm? Let me have you. I hunger for you. Need to be inside you."

Orin was slammed against the wall, his belt unbuckled, pants unzipped, cock exposed before Gavin fell before him, taking his dick down to the root, swallowing him whole. His throat became wrecked from the cries his mate ripped out of him.

"Gavin, oh my. I can't . . . I won't last long. I've been without you too many days after finally having you. Please. Please." Within minutes, Orin came down Gavin's throat, his mate swallowing every drop.

His mate had wrung him out, so it wasn't difficult for Gavin to drag him to his bedroom and throw him down on the bed. Gavin finished pulling his clothes off, leaving Orin lying before his mate, naked and vulnerable. Unbelievably, he was hard again, his skin on fire with need.

"You know, I told Coralia that I wanted you. That I needed you." Gavin removed his clothing. "I've always been submissive, the bottom, but you started a hunger in me that I can't fill without being inside you. I need to be inside you, Orin." He pulled a drawer open beside his bed, retrieving a tube. "I promise not to hurt you."

Orin watched his mate, the way his eyes heated with a fire that seemed to light him up from the inside. The sight left him panting, his body aching. "Hurt me, Gavin. I will take whatever you are willing to give. It matters not to me who is inside whom, only that we are one." He stretched his legs open, presenting his hole to his mate.

Gavin opened the tube quickly, slathering the gel over his long cock. He was sizeable and would truly make an impression inside of Orin's body.

"I can't resist you. Hold your legs up."

Orin immediately did as he was told, his anticipation growing too great to ignore.

"You mentioned claiming. I have my own desire to claim."

Gavin looked at Orin hungrily, deftly handling his cock as he climbed on the bed.

"You're so beautiful, Orin. The moment I saw you, I nearly swallowed my tongue, but I couldn't have you. I thought it would have been a waste for me to try. But you looked my way. You decided I was worthy. And I had to accept that I believed that, too. I need you so much. Need to make you mine. Are you willing to let me have what I need?"

"Yes, Gavin. I had no idea how badly you wanted me."

Gavin slid his hands up and down Orin's legs, touching his thighs before lightly peppering them with kisses.

"Not just want. It is a desperate need I have to fuck you hard and long, come inside you. Make you mine. Is that what you felt like?"

Orin had to admit that he was nervous. It would seem his life was about to change in ways he had not anticipated. "It is exactly how I felt."

Orin watched his mate prepare for him, the hunger devouring him, the tremble in his hands as he settled between Orin's thighs.

"Shit! Haven't gotten you ready yet. Too eager and forgot."

When Gavin prepared to move, Orin placed a hand against his forearm, stopping him.

"No, I'm ready. I can take it, take all of you, Gavin." It would fit, and just as Orin could shift from his merman form to his human one, he knew he could allow his hole to adjust for his mate.

He knew his cock was wet. He could see it standing up, moaning as Gavin tightened his hand around it, stroking up and down.

Orin whimpered. If anything, the pain of Gavin entering his body would be bliss. "You inside me is all I wish for this very moment. Take me."

Gavin took himself in hand again. "You're certain?"

"Please, Gavin. I need you."

Before he'd finished the words, Gavin was pressing forward. His tongue was out and to the side as he thrust inside Orin, who clamped down on the scream fighting to leave his lips.

He felt so full, his wall pulsing, refusing to let Gavin go. His head fell back against the pillow as Gavin reached for his hair, pulling it around in a tight fist while he set a hard-paced rhythm.

"So fucking good, Orin. Your ass is so fucking good. It's tight. Squeezing my dick, sucking it in." Gavin leaned over, snapping his hips forward, rocking back and forth, claiming Orin's body and soul.

"More, Gavin. I had no idea. None. I needed this, need you. More, please."

"Yes, Orin. Just looking at you, watching your eyes glow as I fuck you is a gift. Open your legs wider. I want to get all the way in. I want my balls in your ass. That's it. Beautiful. My dick looks so good going in that ass."

He savored Gavin's kisses, wrapping his arms around Gavin's warm torso as he ravaged him.

"I don't know what's happening to me right now, but I feel myself giving you what we need, what I need to share with you."

"Please, Gavin. Please."

"Tell me you want it."

This was almost like before, except it was Gavin this time, begging him for acceptance, and he would without hesitation.

"I want it. I want everything."

"Yes, that's it. Let's get you turned over. That's what we need to do right now."

Gavin pulled out, and Orin winced. He wasn't ready to let him go, his hole tried to hang on.

Seconds later, he was on his belly, Gavin inside him once more, ramming hip against hip, hand wrapped around Orin's aching cock. Rutting.

"There you go, bring it to me. I'm ready. I don't know what this is, but I'm going to bite you. Please be ready for me. I can't wait."

Orin shouted when Gavin's teeth tore at his neck before suckling his throat. He moaned, his head against his forearms while his mate drank from him. He was getting lightheaded, but he couldn't stop him. Didn't have the energy.

"This is insane, but turn your mouth to me. Taste your blood on my tongue." The kiss was hard and filthy, tongues and teeth and blood, so much of Orin's blood. "There. That's it. Just what I needed. Okay, so I'm going to come now, fill you up with my seed. Here it comes. Oh, fuck yeah, this is it. Do you feel it, Orin? I'm giving you myself. I'm making you a part of me. I needed this. We needed this. Take it."

Orin was drunk on blood, on sex, on the shouts of Gavin's orgasm. Of his own orgasm when Gavin filled his body with his seed, this time coating Orin's insides, and suddenly Orin knew. He knew without a doubt that *he* was the vessel for their young. He felt the connection immediately and closed his eyes, collapsing into the safety of his mate's arms.

"That was so good, Orin, so good. Thank you. Thank you so much. Be ready, going to fuck you again soon. Soon as I wake up, going to stick my dick in your ass and watch you come. Now, who is pregnant? You, right? You have my baby in there? I know you do. I felt it. Will fuck you again when I wake up."

Gavin's dick stayed inside Orin while he slept, pumping Orin's ass full, drenching him on the inside. But Orin didn't move. He was a different person. He was a father carrying a new life. Everything was new, glowing brilliantly.

Gavin intertwined their legs, then placed a hand over Orin's belly.

Orin smiled, setting his hand over his mate's to welcome their young.

Soon, Gavin would wake and take him again, as was the way. Their mating would continue establishing the babe, and Orin would open for him each time.

His mate, father to their young.

Chapter Fifteen

Gavin woke, smiling at the way Orin lay against him, snoring gently with little huffs.

He'd lost count of how many times they'd fucked that night. He couldn't control himself where Orin was concerned. Even now, his dick was hard with just the thought of taking his mate again.

Mate . . . The term seemed old-fashioned, ancient, but then so did Orin. And where did that put him? Here he was, considering a life he'd never envisioned.

And what about Riordan, the man who'd haunted his dreams for so long? How crazy was it that the man had shown up at his home, wanting to apologize? Gavin hadn't believed him and had been prepared to kill the man. Would have, if Orin hadn't shown up.

Orin stretched next to him, reaching over to drag Gavin under him. "You are amazing, my mate."

Gavin smiled into emerald eyes, welcoming Orin's kiss. "So are you."

Orin moaned, then slid his hand down Gavin's inner thigh. "Get on your knees."

Immediately Gavin went to his knees, bending over with an eagerness he felt no reason to hide. He gasped when Orin slapped one cheek, then the other, warming his ass before his tongue slipped inside.

Rocking against Orin's mouth, Gavin begged and pleaded. He nearly came when Orin tugged his cock, surprised he wasn't empty from before. In moments, he was rewarded with the delicious stretch of his hole as Orin took him hard and fast.

After another blazing orgasm, he rested in Orin's arms, tracing circles around Orin's nipples, bending to lick at them, first one and then the other.

Orin lifted Gavin's chin before kissing him and nipping his neck. "I like this."

"You like what?"

"The sharing, the give and take. I haven't enjoyed such pairing before."

Gavin kissed Orin. "Maybe it's because this was meant to be, that you were meant to find me."

"And I am grateful to have found you, Gavin. You are my gift. You have also given me a gift."

Gavin felt his face heat but smiled. "Yes, I felt it. Got you knocked up."

Orin frowned. "Knocked up?"

Gavin loved Orin's confused look, that quirked brow. Orin wore many varied expressions, and Gavin vowed he would learn the meaning behind every one of them.

"So there are some human terms you need to learn, Orin. *Knocked up* means inside you is our child."

Orin kissed Gavin hard. "Yes, touch my belly. Feel our life." He took Gavin's hand and placed it against his stomach. "You are a blessing. I thought myself lacking."

"Lacking?"

Orin sighed. "While I know it is possible for a human to impregnate a merman, I was under the impression that this would not happen to me."

Gavin raised a brow. "Because you're bigger and stronger?"

"Unfortunately, I may have had such thoughts, but I feel I am stronger for being the vessel. The life growing within me is meant to be as I am meant to carry it. I am honored, my heart full, and I have you to thank for this."

"How will this work between us?"

"I had ideas. I wanted to take you to my home, show you my world. But if that isn't what you want, I can learn more about the life you live here. I only wish to be with you, wherever that may be."

"I don't know. Though living in water terrifies me, I think I would like to see what that would be like. I feel like I'm free now, no more shadows hanging over me."

"Riordan?"

"Yes. How often does a person get a chance for closure?"

"Closure?"

Gavin thought for a moment. "Closure is knowing the answer to a life question you've worried about. Like why two people end a relationship, why a parent left, how someone died."

"Interesting. Are they always morbid and fatalistic?"

Gavin smiled. "No, but the answers matter. They're life-changing."

"I see. So, your life was on a path, and you were stuck waiting for this closure?"

Gavin kissed the frown between his mate's eyebrows. "Yes, and now, I want to live. Riordan, for whatever fucked up reason he gave, is gone. Maybe I should have let him go a long time ago, but the mind can be a prison sometimes. And with the closure, it would seem my mind has been freed to do as I wish."

Orion nodded. "It would seem."

"Yes, and instead of running, I'm ready to enjoy our life together. A life with a mystical being who is pregnant with my child is how I want to live."

"Are you certain? This is not a decision you have to make."

Gavin loved how brave Orin was for saying the words but holding onto Gavin tightly as he spoke. No, he didn't want Gavin to go anywhere, and Gavin was going nowhere without him.

"I know. It's one I want to make. I'm ready for an adventure."

"Gavin," Orin hissed when Gavin crawled between his mate's legs and swallowed his dick.

He moaned with pleasure as he savored Orin. He milked Orin dry, squeezing his balls, smiling around his mushroom cap when Orin cried out.

"I want to do this whenever I want." Gavin climbed up to kiss Orin, sharing the taste of his seed. "I want to watch our children grow."

Orin moaned. "You are insatiable."

"Yes, yes I am. "

"You said children."

"Yes, because we will have many. Is that okay with you?"

"I will give you anything you want. Use me."

"I will, Orin."

"Pauric will never believe this."

"Well, let's make sure he does."

Orin sighed when Gavin spread his legs, fucking his way in once more. Orin's eyes rolled back, and he shouted. Gavin grasped Orin's hands tightly, showing him just how well-used he would be.

They left the bedroom hours later to find food. Gavin had a family to care for now and would do his best to do exactly that.

Gavin drove them to the restaurant and insisted on feeding Orin, kissing him between bites.

Tony stood behind the bar, cleaning a glass. "I've seen this look before."

"Yes, you typically share it with me." Adamaris leaned over to kiss Tony.

It wasn't often Gavin saw Adamaris. Life as a lawyer was a busy one. Adamaris spent a lot of time studying for a case or studying with his and Tony's children.

Adamaris smiled at Orin. "Orin, you are looking different,

I'd say. Care to share?"

The blush on his mate's face was a surprise, and he was proud he was the one to put it there.

They'd decided to live in Gavin's home while on land. Gavin made certain Orin was comfortable, touching his belly enough to satisfy his need to connect. The line he felt from his heart to the life growing there amazed him.

"So, you're leaving and moving to Atlantis? And you're okay with this? Not entirely certain how life works there." Tony settled back to listen.

Orin cleared his throat, laughing when Gavin handed him a glass of water. "Thank you, my love."

"Sweet. I love this for you, Orin, and especially for you, Gavin. You seem so much happier, and with how you're caring for Orin, I'm sure you'll have plenty of children." Adamaris held up a wine glass to them before taking a sip.

Orin coughed, spitting the drink he'd sipped onto the bar.

Gavin wiped his lips and refilled his glass. "Watch it, Adamaris, my mate's sensitive about being the one to carry our baby. Now he's said all the right things, but I know he still has thoughts running through that archaic mind of his."

"Careful, Gavin," Orin growled.

"Oh, gonna teach my ass a lesson?"

"Yes, with my hand and then my cock."

"My ears!" Adamaris laughed. "I can't clean those words out of the canals."

Gavin saw how Tony watched Adamaris and knew the two would have a little fun of their own when their children were asleep.

"As to your question, Tony, with me as his guide, Gavin's human body will adjust to meet the needs of our bonding. Already, he is changing, readying himself for the possibility of a life spent in the ocean. But"—Orin paused, glancing at Gavin—"we don't have to remain there or even go home if he wishes to stay. I've told him we may be wherever he wishes."

"Enough, Orin." Gavin snapped. "We're going."

"And we're not," Pauric said, settling beside Orin.

Pauric's hair appeared mussed, his lips swollen. Coralia looked like a bookend, her hair loose and curly, skin flushed from their obvious recent lovemaking.

Orin placed a hand on his friend's shoulder, removing it quickly when both Gavin and Coralia huffed. "I figured as much."

Orin and Pauric shared a grin, clearly satisfied with the protectiveness coming from their mates.

"Oh, no, don't you two get a big head. These are all hormones here, those weird mating things that come about." Coralia's words did nothing to lessen Orin and Pauric's smiles. If anything, they smiled even wider.

"So, I will miss you, my friend, but I'm certain you won't think of me much. You'll be very busy, yes?" Pauric angled his head to indicate Orin's belly, which Gavin lovingly caressed.

"I'll think of you, but yes, I'll be busy."

"We'll be busy," Gavin emphasized.

"Yes, we'll be busy."

Gavin nodded, pleased.

Epilogue

Orin watched as Elion and Selene, his and Gavin's youngest children, sparred. Their movements hinted at the potential of the Guardians they could become, each powerful in their own way. Smiling, he reached into his container, pulling crustaceans and fish from within as he cared for his coral garden. He laughed when their oldest, Marinus, took over, as he often did.

"I've been doing this longer than you have, little one."

"Okay, but I can do it better."

Orin tilted his head. "Can you?"

"Yes. Besides, Father is calling for you."

At that, Orin left Marinus to it. Yes, he still loved his garden, enjoying the vibrant colors and teeming life within. It continued giving him pleasure as he watched it grow.

But his true love was his mate. His treasure. The human who had given them three beautiful children. Even now, Gavin was no doubt planning for more, and Orin was happy to gift him each and every one.

He remembered the day they'd left the surface. Pauric, Coralia, Tony, and Adamaris all stood on the beach to see them off. His men and women rose from the waves as if they'd been waiting for that very moment. His mother had arrived with them, eager to meet his mate and congratulate them on their new life.

Her smile had been knowing, and her embrace of Gavin was one of welcome.

He'd taken his mate, hands joined as they entered the deep surrounded by his, now their people.

As promised, Gavin physically adjusted quickly, though his acclimation to life below the waves took time. Given the time and space he needed, Gavin found his place by helping

Trillian with his art and keeping Graham company. When he came home, they made love and enjoyed their family.

For years—twelve now—he waited nervously for Gavin to decide this wasn't the life for him. Yet his mate enjoyed taking trips, swimming freely, and having what he called watery adventures. And just like their coral garden, they continued to grow.

They had yet to return to the surface, Gavin insisting he'd left nothing behind. He and Coralia used the portal to visit, where Gavin showed off each of their young ones, sharing stories of his watery adventures.

He found his mate in their cell, naked and waiting.

Gavin held out his hand. "Come lay next to me, please."

His mate was as beautiful now as he had been years ago, his skin no less golden, his scales a matching hue. His gorgeous curls fell past his shoulders now, and Orin loved running his fingers through them.

"Of course." Orin drifted to his mate, allowing himself to be embraced.

"You were tending the garden?"

"I was, but I was told you had need of me."

"I do. Our youngest are doing well."

"They are."

"Lay down. Let me taste that sweet ass of yours."

Orin shifted, losing his tail and forming legs. He spread himself open, moaning when Gavin gripped his hips, feeding on his hole. He prepped him, and the sounds he shared blended with Orin's.

Gavin lifted his head, lips puffy, looking into Orin's eyes. "I'm ready for more children. Are you?"

"For you, always, my mate. From now until the end of time."

Other Books by Deja Black:

A Place For Dreams
Getting There
Stumbling in the Dark
They Called Him Nightmare

Broken

Broken Bones
Broken Pieces
Broken Promises
Broken Dreams

Children of the Sun

Flirty and Red

Men of Neptune

Song of the Siren
Guardian's Prize
Life's Greatest Masterpiece
Unbreak My Heart

Tengu Goblins

Challenge the Sun (Part of the Winter Magic Anthology)
Say Yes (Part of Autumn Feast Anthology)
Wink (Part of Spring Fever Anthology)
Beyond the Veil (Part of Summer Heat Anthology)

About the Author

Deja Black had fantasies of men loving men, men who felt strongly, loved hard, and needed a hero. Then one great day, she came across a book and discovered the world of m/m writing, encountered others who shared her obsession as much as she did and found a world where she could not only be accepted for the lives and loves she envisioned, but she could create them too. So why not? Why not take the stories she would write and throw away as a teenager, grow them, dream them, and make them a reality where she could know her characters, let them live their story, and make them real for someone else? And she did. Now, with the support of her hubby and some intense time management, she is learning to balance her family of two energetic children and the many students she counsels each day with her passion for writing what she loves to read.

Deja is always interested in connecting with new people who also share her love, so please feel free to contact her at:
Facebook: www.facebook.com/deja.black.69
Website: dejablack.net
Twitter: @DejaBlack69

About Whitfield Books

Whitfield Books was founded by Steve Whitfield to share stories that capture the spirit of the game and the life lessons it teaches. Built around a love for football, storytelling, and youth development, the brand creates books that inspire young readers to dream big, play with heart, and grow through teamwork and resilience.

The flagship series, *Oakridge FC: The Road to the Final*, follows a youth football team through the highs and lows of tournament football. Each book focuses on a different player, exploring friendship, confidence, and courage both on and off the pitch.

Whitfield Books is about more than sports. It's about community, connection, and character — showing how the values learned on the field can shape who we become beyond it. Discover more stories, character bios, colour scenes and upcoming releases at www.whitfieldbooks.com.

Dedication

For my wife, whose support, patience, and belief make every project possible.

For my sons, Kinnon and Callum. You are my greatest teammates, my proudest moments, and the reason I love this game more every year.

For Max, our Australian Shepherd, who brings endless energy and joy to our home and never misses a chance to chase a ball across the yard.

And for football itself. From muddy pitches on the south coast of England to the all-weather turf fields in Canada, the game has shaped my life, my coaching, and now these stories. This book is a reminder that the journey, the lessons, and the memories we make together matter more than any final score.

About the Author

Steve Whitfield grew up on the south coast of England playing for his local town club and has loved the game ever since. After moving to Canada in 2005, he continued to play and coach, guiding teams and helping young players build confidence, resilience, and teamwork.

He first began coaching after an ACL injury, taking charge of a women's team and guiding them from Division 4 to Division 1 over four seasons. That experience deepened his belief in the power of teamwork, trust, and growth through sport.

Now based in North Vancouver, Steve coaches at North Vancouver Football Club and plays for Seymour FC. His passion for the sport and for inspiring kids both on and off the pitch led him to create *Oakridge FC: The Road to the Final*, a children's football series about courage, friendship, and the lessons learned through the beautiful game.

When he is not coaching or writing, Steve can usually be found watching Premier League matches with his two sons, sketching ideas for new characters, or reflecting on the life lessons sport continues to teach him. Through his writing, he hopes to encourage every young reader to dream big, play with heart, and believe in themselves, both on the field and beyond.

Book 2 Characters

Xavier – Midfield (Captain)
Height: 5'2"
He has a strong, athletic build for his age that makes him stand out the moment he steps onto the field. His skin is a warm brown tone, and his close-cropped black hair is always neatly styled, even after a long practice. He has a calm, focused expression most of the time, with a natural vision that seems to read the game before it happens. Maybe it's the Spanish heritage?

Fun Fact: Has the team record for number of ball juggles in a row - 257 times

Dante – Striker
Height: 5'4"
He is a tall, athletic twelve years old with a bold personality and a quick wit. He's one of the strikers for Oakridge FC and brings a mix of power, flair, and charisma to the pitch. His Italian heritage is evident in his expressive gestures, olive-toned skin, and thick, dark brown hair that's usually swept casually to the side. Dante is known as the jokester of the team.

Fun Fact: Once celebrated a goal with a dance so long the referee told him to get on with the game.

Charles – Winger

Height: 5'1"

Jay's brother and Oakridge's playmaker—balances flair with smart decision-making. They are nearly the same height, making their twin connection clear despite subtle differences in their appearance. Charles has short, tapered hair and a more relaxed smile. His shirt untucked but pinched into his shorts.

Fun Fact: Edits match highlights into mini films that the squad watches on the bus home.

Jay – Winger

Height: 5'1"

Jay is Charles fraternal twin brother! Jay has close-cropped hair and a focused, serious expression. His kit is tidier, shirt tucked, socks pulled high, reflecting his disciplined approach as a right back.

He is a hard-working defender who in known for putting in strong tackles and feeding his brother on the wing.

Fun Fact: Designs custom goal celebrations for every teammate.

Adam – Striker

Height: 5'2"

He is a determined and resilient forward for Oakridge FC, carrying a quiet toughness in his solid, balanced build, strong legs, good posture, and sharp focus. He has ginger hair that curls at the ends, a fair complexion that flushes easily in the sun, and pale blue eyes that constantly scan the field.

Fun Fact: Has a superstition of always putting on his left boot before his right for every match.

Liam - Midfield

Height: 5'1"

He is a quiet, thoughtful twelve-year-old who plays central midfield for Oakridge FC. What he lacks in flash, he makes up for with consistency and intelligence. Liam has light blonde hair parted neatly down the center, fair skin. He rarely raises his voice, but when he does speak, his words carry weight. On the pitch, he's a silent connector, always in the right place, always keeping things moving.

Fun Fact: He once apologized to an opponent *while* stealing the ball from them and then went onto score!

Max – Winger

Height: 5'0"

He might be one of the smallest on the field, but his energy fills every inch of it. A quick, creative winger who can slot in anywhere when the team needs him most, Max brings rhythm both to Oakridge's attack and to the bus rides with his playlist always on cue.

His fearless runs and upbeat spirit make him the spark that keeps Oakridge moving forward.

Fun Fact: Keeps a playlist called 'Final Whistle Joy' that expands after each win.

Sergio – Midfield

Height: 5'5"

Over the past year, Sergio has shot up in height and strength, turning into one of Oakridge's most physical and fastest players. Once a regular on the bench, he's now battling hard for a place in the midfield. With power on his side, the question remains—can he sharpen his skills enough to earn his spot and stay there?

Fun fact: Sergio claims he can eat an entire pizza by himself after every match and usually does.

Coach Torres - Head Coach

Height: 6'1"

He is in his early forties, tall and broad-shouldered, with a steady presence that made people quiet down when he entered a room. He had a short beard that was always neatly trimmed, streaked with just enough gray to make him look wise but not old. His dark hair was cut short and always covered by a black Oakridge FC cap. He usually wore a tracksuit with a whistle hanging from his neck and a stopwatch clipped to his waistband.

Fun Fact: Has a secret collection of match balls from every final he's coached.

Chapter 1:

The Captain's Shadow

Mountain FC 2 – 2 Oakridge FC.

The team jogged into the changing room, some grinning, others still catching their breath. They were damp from the rain, but still in it. The second half would decide everything.

Coach Torres waited until the players had caught their breath and found their seats. He stood in the middle of the changing room, looking each of them in the eye.

"First off, well done," he began. "That was a tough half. We showed heart to come back from two goals down. But we're not done yet."

He turned to the whiteboard again and circled key areas on the pitch.

"They're pushing high on the wings. We need our midfielders to help double up defensively. Jay and Spencer, be vocal. Keep your line tight with Elijah and Aidan."

"Lucas, great penalty save. Keep commanding your box and be ready to play out quickly if they commit numbers forward. Watch for those diagonal switches."

He turned towards Xavier.

"You're the engine. You see everything. Keep our tempo sharp and our shape organised. I want you to find the right moments to drive us forward. Be the link."

The room was silent, the tension rising as the team prepared for the next forty minutes.

Coach Torres looked around one final time, nodding at each boy.

"This is our moment to show who we are. Every second counts. Every decision matters."

He paused, then pointed towards Xavier.

"And now it's your time to lead."

2 weeks earlier …

Xavier stepped out into the crisp morning air, pulling the zipper of his navy and gold Oakridge FC jacket all the way to the top. A thin cloud of breath rose in front of him, quickly vanishing into the quiet. The apartment complex behind him, usually buzzing with the sounds of neighbours and barking dogs, felt unusually still. Even

Mrs. Brenner and her yappy terrier, regular fixtures on the sidewalk at this hour, were nowhere in sight.

He paused at the edge of the walkway, adjusting the straps on his backpack. From inside, the familiar clink of his cleats tapped softly together. He carried them every day, even when there wasn't practice, just in case. The sound was steady and rhythmic, like a heartbeat, reminding him of what mattered most.

Xavier was twelve and already carried himself like someone older. He was strong for his age, with an athletic build and a posture that turned heads the moment he stepped on the pitch. His warm brown skin and neatly cropped black hair gave him a polished, focused look that matched his personality. Calm. Alert. Quietly confident. His eyes always seemed to be scanning the field, reading plays before they happened. Even now, walking to school, he moved with the same controlled, purposeful energy. Everything about him was measured: his stride, his breathing, the way he avoided cracks in the pavement without thinking. His Oakridge FC captain's armband was folded neatly in his jacket pocket, like a badge he didn't need to wear to feel its weight.

The streets were sprinkled with crisp orange and gold leaves, fluttering down from the big maples lining the block. Somewhere a car door slammed. A few blocks away, he heard the distant chatter of kids heading towards Oakridge Middle. He didn't walk with anyone. Not because he didn't have friends; he did, but the quiet suited him. It gave him time to think. And right now, all he could think about was the next match.

Their next opponent: Mountain FC. Tough midfield. High press. Direct balls over the top. Physically strong.

It wasn't going to be easy.

Last weekend's win over Newbridge United had been solid. Lucas had kept a clean sheet, and the front three had clicked. But Xavier hadn't felt great about his own performance. He'd gotten the ball plenty, sure, but he was not happy. His passes hadn't been sharp enough. He hadn't taken control the way a captain should.

And he was the captain. Coach Torres had made that clear.

It hadn't always been like this.

Xavier had been playing football since he was five years old. Back then, the ball looked twice as big as his foot, and the goals were so tiny they could barely fit a kindergartener's dreams. He remembered those early days: tiny fields, Saturday morning orange slices, parents cheering through thermoses of coffee. Even then, he stood out. His coaches always said the same thing.

"Xavier sees the field like a much older player."

"He leads without even trying."

"A natural."

By the time he reached U8, Xavier was already playing with older kids. He stayed a level up for two full seasons, learning to think faster, move smarter, and hold his own against bigger, stronger players. It pushed him to improve quickly, but a part of him missed playing alongside friends his own age.

So, when U10 came around, he returned to his age group. From the very first match, he took command. Xavier ran the midfield like a conductor leading an orchestra, passing with pinpoint accuracy, setting the tempo, and using his voice to direct the flow of the game. He was determined to win, and more often than not, he made it happen. Winning had become second nature.

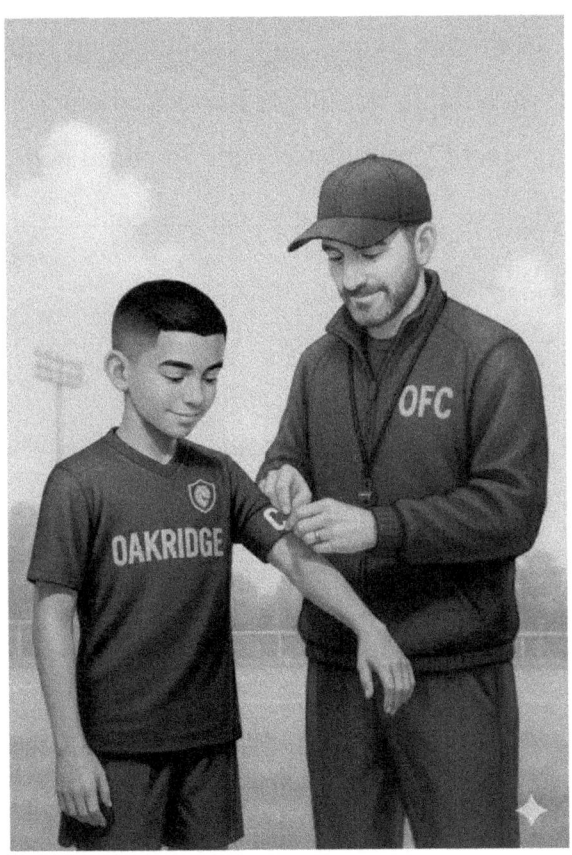

This season at Oakridge wasn't going to be any different. But at the first practice, Coach Torres pulled him aside. For the first time, instead of rotating captains each match, he was naming one permanent captain for the year, and he chose Xavier.

Xavier could barely keep the grin off his face. His heart thudded in his chest, not with nerves but with something more electric, pride maybe, or the feeling of finally stepping into a role he'd always dreamed about.

He'd worn the captain's armband before, but this was different. This wasn't just for one game. This meant the team was his to guide, his to lift up when things got tough, his to lead onto the pitch week after week. It meant Coach trusted him. The team could trust him.

But even the excitement of being captain couldn't shake the tired feelings he was having.

Not on the surface. Xavier was sharp in training, first to arrive and last to leave. But inside, there was a different kind of tired. Not the kind that came from sprinting drills or long matches. A quieter kind. The kind that came from switching lives every week.

His parents had split when he was nine. They sat him down together and explained it calmly. It wasn't about him. They still cared about each other, but they needed to live apart. He remembered nodding through it all, not really knowing what it would mean.

Now, years later, he was used to the routine: one week with Mum, one week with Dad. Two condos, two beds, two laundry baskets. They didn't live far from each other, and they got along well enough. No yelling, no awkward silences. Just separate lives.

It wasn't bad. But it wasn't easy either.

Sometimes he forgot where he'd left his maths book. Sometimes he missed little things, like waking up to the same kitchen every day. And sometimes, even though he had both of them in his life, he just felt a little bit in between.

Football helped with that. The field didn't care whose week it was. There was only one ball, one team, one game.

And that was enough.

So, he threw himself into the game.

Football is life!

Xavier arrived at school just before the bell. He passed Dante in the hallway; he was a good friend from Oakridge and a tall, fast, all-energy player. He gave him a quick nod. Dante grinned and tossed him a fist bump.

"Captain," he said with a smirk. "Ready to run things this weekend?"

"Always," Xavier said.

Behind Dante, Liam appeared from the stairwell, hoodie up, backpack dragging. Quiet as usual. Liam wasn't flashy, but he had solid positioning and an eye for space. Xavier liked playing with him. Reliable. Tactical.

"Hey," Xavier called. "Don't forget to bring your shin guards today."

Liam nodded wordlessly and ducked into their shared homeroom.

Xavier shook his head. Liam had potential, but he was too passive. If Oakridge was going to beat Mountain FC, they needed more than quiet reliability. They needed intensity. Control. Command.

That's what Xavier would bring.

That afternoon's practice was intense. Coach Torres set up a high-tempo scrimmage designed to test quick reactions and control under pressure. The midfield was a whirlwind of movement, navy and bright green pinnies darting through tight spaces.

Coach Torres was in his early forties, tall and broad-shouldered, with a steady presence that made people quiet down when he entered a room. He had a short beard that was always neatly trimmed, streaked with just enough grey to make him look wise but not old. His dark hair was cut short and always covered by a faded navy Oakridge FC cap. He usually wore a tracksuit with a whistle hanging from his neck and a stopwatch clipped to his waistband. His eyes were sharp and serious, but kind too; like he saw everything happening on and off the pitch, even when you thought he wasn't looking.

Xavier called out constantly, directing players like chess pieces.

"Charles, shift left!"

"Dante, overlap!"

"Lucas, push the back line higher!"

But not everyone was listening. Charles, the right back, rolled his eyes after the third instruction.

"Relax, Xavier. We get it."

Xavier felt a flicker of irritation.

"If you'd marked your man last week, I wouldn't have to keep reminding you."

"Seriously?" Charles snapped. "We won the game."

Coach Torres blew the whistle hard.

"Cut the chatter!" he barked. "If you've got feedback, save it for the debrief. Play on!"

The ball restarted, but the tension didn't disappear. Xavier's voice was quieter now. Inside, though, he was boiling.

Why didn't they get it? Being captain didn't mean bossing people around; it meant knowing what needed to happen before anyone else did. Seeing the whole picture.

After practice, Coach Torres pulled him aside.

"Walk with me," the coach said.

They strolled along the sideline in silence for a moment.

"You're doing a good job, Xavier," he began. "But I can see the pressure weighing on you."

Xavier frowned. "I just want us to be ready. Mountain's no joke."

"I know. But sometimes leadership is about letting others step into the moment. Give them space to grow."

"I'm trying," Xavier muttered.

Coach Torres stopped and turned to him.

"I know you are. But being captain doesn't mean commenting on every play or carrying the whole team on your back. Let the others figure some things out on their own. Think about who on this team needs a voice… who's waiting for permission to lead alongside you?"

Xavier didn't answer. Not right away.

"Not everyone has been playing for as long as you. Encourage and support," Coach Torres said as he patted him on the back.

Maybe he was talking about Lucas. Or Charles. Or maybe even Dante, who was already starting to be the focal point for the attack. Either way, it was something to think about.

Xavier stayed behind after practice longer than usual. As the last cones were stacked and the goals wheeled off, he lingered on the edge of the pitch, stretching out tight calves that had nothing to do with sore muscles.

Life off the pitch had its own kind of challenge.

When he stayed with his mum for the week, everything ran like clockwork. She was organised, efficient, always juggling work and life. After practice, she'd pick him up in her SUV, usually with a protein bar waiting in the cupholder. Dinners were quick but healthy: stir fry, wraps, rice bowls, and then she'd disappear into her home office for a Zoom meeting while he finished homework at the kitchen table. The condo was tidy, his bed always made, and the fridge labelled with meals for each day. Calm, steady, predictable.

A week with his dad felt different. More relaxed. Less structured. They might order takeout two nights in a row or watch a match while eating on the couch. His dad let him stay up later, especially if there was Champions League on, and they'd sometimes talk through the tactics like pundits, pausing the game to debate a formation. His room at Dad's wasn't quite as neat, but it was full of energy: match programmes, old jerseys, a mini whiteboard where he'd draw line-ups for fun. It felt more like a football zone than a bedroom.

Both weeks had their own rhythm. One quiet and efficient. The other loose and full of banter. He loved them both, but switching between them made it hard to feel settled. Like he was always adjusting, always adapting. Only on the pitch did everything feel consistent: one team, one goal, one version of himself.

It wasn't bad. In fact, compared to other kids he knew, it was about as smooth as it could be. His parents still got along. They both showed up for his matches. They texted each other politely if he left a book at the wrong place.

It worked.

Most of the time.

But even when everything was "fine", it still wore on him. Little things, like forgetting which apartment had his shin pads, or which fridge had his favourite cereal. Some days, he just wanted one place to come home to. Not because either parent wasn't trying, but because bouncing back and forth made him feel like he was always in motion, never settled.

He didn't talk about it much. Not with Coach. Not with teammates. Not even with Dante (his best friend) or Liam (his midfield partner). Xavier was an only child, and he'd always been good at handling things on his own. Practising free kicks for hours. Writing out his own meal plans. Keeping his room organised no matter which home he was in.

He'd tried once with Dante, a few weeks ago, but the words caught in his throat.

How do you even start a conversation like that?

Hey, my parents are divorced and can I talk to you about it...? No, how could he relate?

So instead, he trained harder. Studied formations. Cleaned his cleats. Took control of everything he could. Because if he couldn't fix things at home, maybe he could still fix things on the pitch.

But some days, like this one, he wished someone else really got it. What it felt like to lead a team, stay on top of school, and carry two homes in your head at once.

He adjusted his socks, stood, and looked out across the empty field. It was the only place that felt like one version of his life. One identity, no switching.

Just the game.

And for now, that was enough.

That night, Xavier sat at his desk, laptop open but untouched. His homework lay forgotten as he watched clips from Oakridge's last match. He paused on one scene: Liam laying off a smart first-touch pass that set up their second goal. Nobody had noticed it in the moment.

But Xavier had.

He made a mental note to bring it up tomorrow.

A light knock sounded at his bedroom door. His mum peeked in.

"Lights out soon, okay?"

"Yeah."

She hesitated.

"How you feeling about the tournament?"

He nodded. "Okay. We've got a good chance this year."

"Love you." She left, and the silence grew thick again.

He turned back to the laptop, but instead of homework, he opened a new tab and searched Kevin De Bruyne highlights. The Belgian maestro had always been one of his favourites. Clinical. Calm. Always a step ahead.

Xavier watched in silence as the screen flickered to life with smooth passes, perfect vision, and impossible assists.

For a moment, everything faded: the pressure, the expectations, the worry.

Just football.

Just the game he loved.

And the captain he still wanted to become.

Chapter 2:

Fault Lines

Xavier didn't sleep much that night.

His eyes stayed open long after midnight, fixed on the shadows dancing across his ceiling. His laptop still sat open on his desk, looping highlights of Manchester City's 2023 title run. De Bruyne to Haaland. A no-look pass. A curling assist. Perfect weight, perfect angle. Again and again.

He knew every touch, every movement. The game made sense in a way nothing else did right now.

Xavier's bedroom at his mum's condo was small but spotless, just like the rest of the apartment. The walls were painted a soft grey, with a single framed photo of him holding a Man of the Match trophy from last season hanging above his desk. His bed was always neatly made, usually by his mum before he even got home from school, with dark blue sheets and a folded Oakridge FC blanket at the foot. A narrow bookshelf stood in the corner, lined with school binders, a few football biographies, and a framed photo of him with

Coach Torres and the team. His desk was organised, with his laptop docked in the corner and a small lamp for late-night homework sessions. His cleats sat by the door, always cleaned and ready, and his match-day bag hung from a hook on the wall. It was a quiet space. Tidy. Focused. Almost like a hotel room made just for training and school, but sometimes it felt like something was missing. It was his room, but not quite him.

The next morning, Xavier got up before his alarm. He pulled on his Oakridge FC hoodie, the soft navy fabric stretched slightly at the sleeves from years of wear. It was his lucky hoodie; he'd had it since U9s. It still fit. Kind of. He was a little superstitious, though he'd never admit it out loud. He'd worn it during his best matches, and not bringing it on game day just felt wrong. He also had a ritual of cleaning his boots the night before each match, scrubbing every bit of mud off with an old toothbrush and laying them side by side under his desk, perfectly aligned. He told himself it was just routine, part of being prepared, but deep down he believed those little habits helped him feel ready, like they gave him control over something when everything else in life felt uncertain.

Breakfast was quiet, as usual.

His mum sipped coffee at the kitchen island, scrolling her phone. Her work badge hung from the corner of her bag.

"Morning," she said, without looking up.

"Morning," Xavier replied.

He poured a bowl of cereal and sat across from her. The only sound was the rhythmic tapping of her thumb on the screen.

"You need a ride today?" she asked finally.

Xavier shook his head. "I'm walking. Got my cleats for after school."

She nodded and put her phone down. For a second, she looked at him the way she used to, like she was seeing him, not just checking off a box.

"You okay, Xav?"

He hesitated. Something inside him wanted to say *No*. To tell her how much he missed things the way they were. But instead, he said, "Yeah. Just focused on the game this weekend."

She smiled, but it didn't reach her eyes.

"I know you are. You always are."

He grabbed his bag and stood up.

"Love you," he said.

"Love you too," she answered, already turning her focus back to work.

At school, Xavier moved through the day like clockwork: maths, history, lunch, science. He barely heard the lectures. His mind was on Mountain FC. Their centre-mids were physical and fast. If Oakridge gave them time on the ball, they'd get punished. He needed to find a way to break their rhythm early.

At lunch, he sat with Lucas, Charles, Jay and Liam. Dante was late as usual, balancing a tray with three cookies and a can of Red Bull.

"Nutrition of champions," Charles muttered, raising an eyebrow.

Dante shrugged. "If it works, it works."

Xavier leaned over to Liam. "You remember how Mountain played last year?"

Liam nodded. "They overload the left side. Their number 8 drifts wide, pulls defenders out of shape."

Xavier smiled. "Exactly what I remember. We can trap him if we press right."

Charles overheard and groaned. "You two already doing match breakdowns at lunch?"

Xavier raised an eyebrow. "You'd know more if you joined us yesterday."

"I was doing homework," Charles said flatly.

Dante shot Xavier a quick glance. A warning. Let it go.

Xavier bit his tongue and turned back to Liam. "We'll need to stay compact. You and me, we control the middle. That's how we win."

Liam gave a small nod. "I'm ready."

It was the kind of answer that used to annoy Xavier. Too soft. Too neutral. But today, it sounded steady. Grounded. Like maybe Liam was just quiet, not uncertain.

Maybe Coach was right. Maybe other voices just needed space.

After school, practice was all about "shape", as Coach Torres called it. He meant the team's formation, where everyone was on the field.

Coach Torres divided them into units: defensive line, midfield triangle, attacking third. Xavier and Liam ran patterns together for nearly forty minutes, sharpening their timing, spacing and communication.

"Play it early," Xavier said. "Let me run onto it."

Liam nodded and delivered a clean pass into the gap between cones.

"Better," Xavier said. "Now again. First touch this time."

They went through it again. And again. And again.

Across the pitch, Coach Torres stood with his arms crossed, watching silently.

After the session, the team huddled around him for debrief.

"Mountain FC will push us hard," the coach said. "Their press isn't pretty, but it works. They force errors. So, we counter that with discipline. Intelligence. Focus."

He looked around at each player, making eye contact.

"But most of all… we stay united. Trust the guy next to you. Know your job, and trust him to do his."

His eyes landed on Xavier last.

"Captain, anything to add?"

Xavier looked around the group. Every face was watching, expecting, trusting.

He took a deep breath.

"We've worked too hard to let pressure shake us. If we stay tight, we'll win. But only if we work together. Every player, every run, every challenge. No shortcuts."

Heads nodded. A few mutters of agreement rippled through the group.

Coach smiled. "That's what I like to hear."

As the players broke away at the end of practice, Lucas walked over, picking up a ball on the way. "See you tomorrow, Xavier!"

"Yeah," Xavier said, remembering when Lucas first joined the team. He'd been quiet, almost shy, hanging near the edge of the group during warm-ups and drills, barely saying a word. Some of the other boys had overlooked him in the tryouts; he wasn't the tallest, and goalkeepers didn't always get the spotlight unless they made a big save. But Xavier had made an effort from day one of him joining the team. He'd passed Lucas the ball first during drills, clapped for him even when he missed a save, and always said something encouraging when he looked unsure. "Good hands," he'd say, or "Nice positioning," even if Lucas had just picked the ball out of the net. Xavier had seen something in him: reflexes, discipline, quiet determination. Lucas wasn't just the goalie. He was *their* goalie now. And with the right support, Xavier knew he could be great for Oakridge.

He felt this was the captain's job: make the new players feel welcome. There hadn't been many weeks for them to settle into the team before the tournament started, and they had to be a team if they were going to go far. The best team.

After practice, Dante trotted over and gave a friendly slap on the back.

"You good?" he asked.

Xavier looked at him. "What do you mean?"

Dante shrugged. "You been on edge. Even for you."

Xavier bent to pick up a cone. "Just focused."

"You sure?"

Xavier didn't answer right away. Then: "Things at home are… weird. I don't like switching between Mum and Dad every week. I feel like I have to hold everything together."

Dante nodded slowly. "Yeah. That's tough."

Xavier looked at his cleats. "The pitch is the only place that still feels normal."

"I get that," Dante said. "But even captains need a break."

Xavier almost laughed. "There are no breaks. Not now. We win this next match, we're through. We lose, and we're in trouble."

Dante smiled faintly. "You sound like Coach."

"Maybe I'm turning into him."

Dante patted his shoulder again. "Just don't start growing a beard!"

That got a chuckle. For the first time in days.

Xavier and Dante had been teammates for a few years, but it wasn't until last season that they started to grow close. On the surface, they were opposites. Xavier was serious and focused, while Dante was bold and energetic, always cracking jokes and bringing the locker room to life. Dante played as a striker, and everything about him was fast: his feet, his first touch, even the way he talked. He had short, curly hair that bounced when he ran and a grin that made it hard to stay mad at him, even when he missed an easy chance. He wore flashy boots and never tied them the same way twice, insisting it gave him more "freedom". But under all that swagger was a smart player who timed his runs with precision and knew how to create space.

During away games, Dante and Xavier's parents took turns to drive them, and Dante's father used to play the music really loud when it was his turn. They loved it. When they stopped at traffic lights, especially when there were people around, he would bring the windows down to embarrass the boys. But Dante thrived as the centre of attention and would sing at the top of his lungs whatever was on. Xavier was a little shy, but as they drove away, they would all be laughing and talking about the looks they had got all the way to the game.

That night, Xavier sat at the kitchen table with his cleats, gently cleaning the dirt from the studs with an old toothbrush. It was his routine. A ritual. The only way he could calm his brain before a big game.

His mum passed by on the way to the laundry room. She paused.

"Still cleaning those by hand, huh?"

Xavier nodded. "Makes me feel ready."

She leaned against the counter. "You've always taken care of your gear. Even when you were five years old. You used to sleep in your first jersey, remember?"

He smiled. "It was itchy."

"You refused to take it off for days. You said you wanted to be a professional player."

Xavier picked the last bits of mud from the sole.

"I still want to be one."

His mum walked over and kissed the top of his head.

"You will be."

He didn't say anything, but for the first time all week, he felt the edge of the pressure ease.

Just a little.

Chapter 3:

Cracks in the Game Plan

Thursday afternoon practice felt more like a test than a tune-up. The sun was low and golden across the Oakridge FC training pitch, casting long shadows over cones, bibs and goals. Coach Torres had laid out a possession drill in a tight 20x20 grid. The midfielders — Xavier, Liam, Max and Charles — were locked in a three-touch game against the defenders. Quick play. Fast decisions. Minimal space.

Xavier thrived in drills like these. Or at least, he used to.

Now, every bad touch felt personal.

"Faster!" he barked after Charles took one too many steps. "You're killing the rhythm."

Charles scowled. "Maybe call for the ball next time instead of acting like a coach."

Coach Torres blew the whistle once. "Keep moving! Reset positions!"

Liam passed the ball wide and Max flicked it back inside, but Xavier cut it off, sticking a leg out behind him.

"Don't force it," he snapped. "You've got the reverse angle open."

Max rolled his eyes. "Not everyone's got X-ray vision, man."

Another whistle. Another reset. Another crack forming.

From the sideline, Lucas stood in his keeper kit, stretching against the goalpost. He saw it. Everyone did. The cohesion that had lifted them through pre-season and the first match was starting to fray.

And the more it frayed, the tighter Xavier gripped the reins.

After practice, Coach Torres pulled Xavier aside. Again.

They stood near the equipment shed, the sound of cleats crunching gravel fading behind them.

"You want to win, Xavier. I see that. And I respect it."

Xavier nodded cautiously.

"But you're trying to manage everything. Teammates. Tempo. Tactics. Emotion. That's not leadership. That's control."

Xavier looked down.

"I'm just trying to get it right," he muttered.

"Getting it right doesn't mean doing it alone. You're not a solo act. This isn't tennis."

Xavier stayed quiet. A breeze picked up, tree branches swaying and leaves fluttering to the ground.

"I know things are complicated off the pitch," Coach said. "You don't have to say anything, but I see it."

That caught Xavier off guard.

Coach Torres wasn't the type to pry. He didn't do personal heart-to-hearts. But there was something in his tone — calm, firm, knowing — that struck a chord.

"Just remember," Coach said, "football's not about controlling every little thing. I get that things at home might feel out of your hands, but don't bring that weight out here. On the pitch, you've got to trust your teammates. Let go a little. That's what makes it the beautiful game."

As practice was winding down, Xavier was doing kick-ups near the touchline with Lucas. They weren't really talking, just trading little tricks and trying to outlast each other. But Xavier's ears perked up when he heard his mum's voice nearby. She had come a few minutes early for pickup and was speaking quietly with Coach Torres near the bench.

"How's he doing?" she asked, her voice low but audible.

Coach paused before answering. "He's focused. Maybe a little too focused lately. He's taking on a lot. More than most kids his age would."

There was a silence. Then Coach added, "Nothing bad. He's just... pushing himself hard. You can see it in how he trains. It's like he's trying to control everything all at once."

His mum sighed. "Yeah. Things at home have been... complicated."

Coach nodded. "He's a great kid. Smart. Responsible. I've had a few chats with him. He listens."

"Well," she said, "thank you for talking to him. Me and his father appreciate it. You're great with him, he really listens to you!"

Xavier kept his eyes on the ball, pretending not to hear, but he wasn't sure if he felt embarrassed or grateful. Maybe both. But something about hearing them talk, knowing someone else saw what he was dealing with, made him feel just a little less alone.

That night, Xavier sat on the floor of his room, his whiteboard angled in front of him. He'd drawn Mountain FC's formation from memory: 4-2-3-1. Their left mid, number 11, was an aggressive player. He often moved inside instead of going down the wing. Liam would have to cover more ground on that side.

He uncapped a blue marker and drew arrows from Liam's position to the right channel. Then erased it. Then drew a new angle.

A knock on the door pulled him out of his thoughts.

His dad.

"Hey," his dad said, stepping in. "You ready to go to mine, bud?"

Xavier put the marker down.

"Sure."

His dad looked tired. His tie was still on but loose, and his shirt sleeves were wrinkled.

"Be safe, see you at the game this weekend," his mum said as they walked towards the elevators in the apartment complex.

"Bye, Mum, love you," Xavier said.

Xavier's dad kept the elevator door open and he walked in.

"How's training been this week?" he asked as the door closed.

"Not bad. Coach is helping me be a better captain. It's so hard when some of the players are new and just don't get it," Xavier said.

"They will catch up quick, show them how it's done!" his dad said, as the elevator reached the ground floor and they headed to the car.

At school the next day, the tension spilled over.

During lunch, the team grabbed a quiet table at the edge of the cafeteria. Liam sat next to Xavier, unpacking a sandwich wrapped in foil. Jay and Charles had been arguing about something that happened in the last game against Newbridge United.

"I'm telling you, you didn't track back fast enough," Jay said, jabbing a piece of carrot with his fork. "That's why their winger got through."

Charles rolled his eyes and dropped his tray onto the table with a thud. "Are you serious? I was marking two players because you drifted out of position. Go watch the replay."

"Oh, come on," Jay snapped. "I was covering midfield like Coach said. You always think it's someone else's fault."

"That's because it usually is," Charles muttered, arms folded across his chest.

Dante laughed, biting into a cookie. "You two fight more than my cousins."

"Well, we *are* brothers, Dante!" Charles and Jay said in unison.

Lucas looked to Xavier for a calming word. But Xavier was staring down at his lunch tray, unmoved.

"Guys, cool it," he finally said.

Jay leaned in. "You don't control this one, Xavier!"

That surprised Xavier. The table went quiet.

"What's that supposed to mean?" he asked.

Jay shrugged. "Just saying. You don't have to micromanage every breath we take."

Xavier's jaw clenched. "Just trying to help. We win because we're organised. Because we *are* a team. You think we'll beat Mountain with playground football?"

Dante put a hand on Xavier's shoulder. "Let's cool off. Save it for the pitch."

Xavier stood and grabbed his tray.

"Fine," he muttered. "Just don't blame me when we get steamrolled because nobody listens."

He dumped the tray and walked out of the cafeteria, heart pounding.

That evening, Xavier didn't watch any highlights. Didn't review any formations. He sat in the courtyard of the apartment complex with his ball and juggled in silence, eyes on the grass.

He lost count after eighty-seven touches.

When he finally stopped, the sun was almost gone, the sky painted in pale orange and fading violet.

"Dinner's ready." His dad had leaned over the balcony a few floors up.

"I'm not hungry," he said.

He hesitated, then nodded.

Xavier sat there another twenty minutes. Alone. Listening to the wind in the trees, trying to let go of the weight he carried.

He wasn't sure how.

But for once, he wanted to try.

Xavier was hungry now. A cheese sandwich and sliced apples awaited inside, one of his favourites.

Chapter 4:

Pressure Cooker

Coach Torres wasn't holding back.

Friday afternoon practice was short, sharp and soaked with intensity. The match against Mountain FC was tomorrow, and every player could feel it.

Oakridge FC trained in two units, defensive and midfield versus attacking wave. Coach set up a half-pitch press-and-break drill: midfielders had to resist a simulated high press and build forward with limited touches. One mistake and the attackers pounced.

Xavier barked instructions nonstop, a machine of motion and voice.

"Liam, shift sooner!"

"Jay, tuck inside before they close the lane!"

"Charles, now, not three seconds from now!"

After fifteen minutes, Coach blew the whistle and waved everyone in.

"Water break. Two minutes."

Xavier stayed at the top of the drill zone, hands on hips, frustration burning behind his eyes.

Jay came over, not bothering to hide his irritation. "You realise we're not robots, right?"

Xavier didn't even look at him. "You want to get pressed into the ground tomorrow?"

"I want to play without getting screamed at every time I blink."

Liam stepped between them, calm as ever. "Let's cool it."

Xavier opened his mouth but stopped. He looked past them, towards the benches, where Lucas was talking to Coach Torres.

Jay walked off, shaking his head. Liam lingered a moment.

"You're trying to do the right thing," Liam said. "Just… maybe not the right way."

Then he was gone too.

Xavier sat on the turf and pulled his shin guards off. His legs felt heavy. Not from training, but from everything else. He was frustrated. Was it the pressure of being the captain?

And the game hadn't even started.

However, that night was a chance to relax and have fun. Dante was coming over, and he was excited for that.

Xavier and Dante sat cross-legged on the carpet in Xavier's room, controllers in hand, eyes locked on the glowing TV screen. The air was filled with the sound of rapid button clicks, roaring virtual crowds and their own laughter bouncing off the walls.

Xavier had picked Manchester City, his favourite team of course, while Dante, always the wildcard, went with Southampton just to prove a point. "Underdog magic," he grinned. Despite the lopsided match-up, Dante was dominating. He was ridiculously good at EA Sports FC, pulling off skill moves and no-look passes like he was actually on the pitch. Xavier groaned as another goal slid past Ederson. "There's no way you practised this much," he said, half-laughing. Dante just shrugged, eyes glued to the screen. "Talent, bro. Can't teach it."

For once, the pressure melted away. No captain's armband, no family stress. Just two friends, a pile of snacks and a beautiful game they both loved.

As the match continued, their playing styles couldn't have been more different. Xavier was trying to build slow, elegant attacks: one-touch passes through the midfield, triangle movements, perfectly timed through balls. It was how he dreamed Oakridge FC would play. Fluid, composed, like the City teams he watched on repeat.

Dante, on the other hand, was pure chaos. He'd launch long balls from his centre backs, attempt bicycle kicks with defenders who had no business even being in the box, and constantly tried flicks and spins with players whose in-game stats definitely didn't support it. "Bro, why is your left back doing stepovers?" Xavier laughed, shaking his head. "Just wait," Dante grinned, mashing the buttons, "he's got a goal in him, I swear." It was ridiculous, unpredictable and completely fun, and for Xavier, it was exactly the kind of break he didn't realise he needed.

It was getting late, and Dante had finally left after a marathon of video games. The house felt quieter without his constant commentary, just the low hum of the TV in the background. Xavier flopped onto the couch beside his dad, who was already halfway through a mug of tea and watching the post-match highlights from the Premier League.

On the screen, a familiar voice cut through the studio noise. Roy Keane. Former Manchester United captain, now commentator.

His dad nodded toward the TV. "Now there's a captain," he said with a grin. "Roy Keane. Hard as nails. Didn't care who you were, he held everyone to the same standard."

Xavier smirked. "You and your United stories again."

His dad chuckled. "What can I say? Best days of football there ever were. Keane, Scholes, Giggs, Beckham… that was a team that meant business."

Xavier leaned forward, resting his elbows on his knees as the highlights rolled. "What made Keane so good as captain?"

His dad took a sip of tea and thought for a moment. "He wasn't just loud. He was clear. When he spoke, people listened because he backed it up every single time. He played like it mattered, no matter who the opponent was. You could see it in his eyes — total focus."

Xavier's gaze lingered on the screen. Keane was mid-sentence, talking about leadership, the importance of standards and not letting emotions get in the way.

"Your mum says I talk too much about football," his dad said with a grin. "But this stuff matters. Keane didn't just tell players what to do — he showed them. That's what made him great."

"I want to be a better captain," Xavier said quietly. "Coach made me captain for the season, but it feels like I'm trying too hard. Like I'm controlling everything instead of leading."

His dad nodded slowly. "That's normal. Everyone thinks being captain means taking charge of every moment. But the best captains, like Keane, they don't try to do everything themselves. They trust the players around them. They let people figure things out but are always ready to lift them up when it goes wrong."

Xavier turned to face him. "But what if they let me down?"

"Then you pick them back up," his dad said, matter-of-factly. "That's what captains do."

The two sat in silence for a while, the TV flickering soft light across the room. Another replay rolled. Keane shared his opinions on the play, pointing out a lack of effort. "I'd be livid if he was on my team," he said.

His dad leaned back on the couch. "You know, he captained United through their best years. Seven league titles, four FA Cups, a Champions League. He wasn't the flashiest, but he was the heartbeat. Every man on that team knew exactly what he expected from them. And it started with how he carried himself."

He glanced at Xavier. "That's your job too. You don't have to be the loudest. You just have to be the heartbeat."

The game highlights faded into commercials. His dad stretched and stood, setting his mug in the sink.

"Alright, captain," he said, smiling at the nickname. "Tomorrow, don't try to control the game. Command it. There's a difference."

Xavier sat back against the couch, eyes still on the now-dark TV screen. He could still hear Keane's voice echoing faintly in his head, calm but certain. He leaned forward, picking up the remote. For a moment, he thought about turning the TV back on, watching another replay of the match. Instead, he just sat there, the captain's armband draped over the armrest beside him.

Tomorrow wasn't just another game.

It was his chance to show who he was — not just with the ball at his feet, but with the trust of ten teammates behind him.

He smiled faintly, stood and turned off the lamp. The glow from the streetlights spilled across the Oakridge crest on his training jacket as he whispered to himself,

"Time to lead."

Chapter 5:

Halftime Shift

Xavier stepped out of the car into the cool morning air, his boots already laced, his hoodie zipped up over his jersey. The clouds overhead were thick and grey, drifting slow and heavy across the sky. There was the faint smell of damp grass and a hint of rain in the breeze. Perfect football weather, he told himself.

He walked beside Liam toward the changing rooms, not saying much. Inside, the atmosphere was already tense, focused. Coach Torres was waiting by the whiteboard with his marker in hand. No music. No small talk. Just the quiet buzz of players mentally preparing.

"Today's going to be a battle," Coach began, underlining *Mountain FC* in big block letters. "They're stronger, more physical, and they press hard. But that doesn't mean we let them control the tempo."

Xavier locked in immediately, his eyes following every line Coach drew on the board. It was the same shape they'd used before, *4-4-2*, but with a few tactical tweaks.

Subs: Leo, Fabian, Sergio, Ben, Ryan

"Same shape. Same instructions. But I want quicker passes from the back, especially when we're under pressure. Lucas, you're going to be more involved today. Expect to use your feet. Build from the back."

Xavier glanced at Lucas, who gave a short nod.

"Xavier," Coach continued, "keep the midfield organised. Talk constantly. Max, stretch their back line. Dante, hold it up when needed."

It was what Xavier had been waiting for, not just the words, but the moment. The air before kick-off. The weight of responsibility. He felt steady. Focused. Ready.

Coach closed with a simple line that hit Xavier hard: "This match will test us. Mentally. Physically. But that's what we want. That's how we grow."

And then they were walking out. The parents were mainly on one side of the pitch, clustered near two tents. Patches of blue sky peeked through the clouds, but dark ones still hovered. The rain hadn't come yet, but it would.

Xavier pulled his jersey tight, bounced on his toes and looked across the field at Mountain FC. Big. Confident. Ready.

But so was he.

He was ready to lead. He adjusted his captain's armband and went out to command the game.

The changing room door closed behind them with a thud.

Jerseys clung to damp skin. Rain had stopped, but the storm inside the game hadn't. Boots squeaked against the tiled floor. Most of the boys slumped onto the benches, catching their breath. Others paced. Dante had already taken his shirt halfway off, steam rising from his shoulders.

Xavier sat down slowly, eyes fixed on the floor. His legs were burning, his chest still rising and falling with each breath. That half had been chaos — beautiful, painful chaos.

From 2–0 down to 2–2. And not just any equaliser. A header from Dante. A sharp finish from Adam. And a save — that penalty save — from Lucas just before the whistle.

Xavier could still hear the Oakridge parents' roar in his ears.

Coach Torres stood in the middle of the room, arms crossed. He waited until every player had settled in, then began.

"First off, well done. That was a tough half. We showed heart to come back from two goals down. But we're not done yet."

He turned towards the whiteboard, already marked up from before kick-off. He circled areas on the left and right flanks.

"They're pushing high on the wings. Jay and Spencer, you need to stay sharp. Talk to your centre backs. Elijah and Aidan, you've done well clearing pressure, but we need to stay tighter as a unit."

Lucas stood up straighter as Coach looked his way.

"Lucas, that penalty save — huge. Stay switched on. Keep communicating with your back line. If they press hard again, play short and smart. Don't rush. Let us build."

Lucas gave a small nod, his face calm but proud. Xavier could tell the save had given him a boost. He'd earned it.

Then Coach looked directly at Xavier.

"And you — you're the engine. You see everything. Shape, tempo, space. Keep our midfield organised and start our attacks with intent. Be patient, but when you see a moment to break forward, take it. We trust your read."

Xavier swallowed and nodded. Weight on his shoulders, but hearing those words sparked something. He remembered his dad talking about Roy Keane; the conversation echoed in his mind. *You don't control the game. You command it.*

Coach took a step back and swept his gaze across the room.

"This second half will decide everything. They'll come out fast. They want to knock us off balance again. So, stay calm. Win the first five minutes, then make them chase us."

The boys nodded. A quiet energy began to rise. Aidan slapped Elijah's shoulder. Max laced his boots tighter. Adam cracked his knuckles and rolled his neck.

Coach pointed at Xavier one last time.

"This is your moment to lead. You've been preparing for it since last season. Now it's here."

Xavier stood slowly. His jersey was still soaked. His boots felt heavier than usual. But none of that mattered. He was the heart; he would show the way forward.

He looked around the room. Lucas, steady as ever. Liam, quietly focused. Dante, buzzing with energy. Elijah, ready to prove himself. They were all looking back at him.

He didn't need a speech.

"Let's go win the second half."

They stood there in unison. "Let's go!" the team shouted back.

And as they walked back out into the light drizzle and the noise of the crowd in anticipation for the second half, Xavier could feel it.

This was his moment to lead.

Chapter 6:

Commanding the Middle

The whistle blew, and the second half began.

Xavier stepped onto the pitch with soaked boots and a clear mind. The field felt heavier after the rain, the grass damp beneath his studs, but everything else felt lighter.

The crowd noise picked up again as Mountain FC pressed high, just like they had in the first half. Their number 6 was barking orders, clapping his hands, trying to rattle Oakridge's shape.

But Xavier wasn't rattled.

"Liam, tuck in left. Jay, don't chase — hold that line," he called, eyes scanning the field. "Let's move it quick."

Elijah received the ball under pressure and passed it square to Aidan. Aidan took a touch, then played it into midfield where Xavier met it, opening his body to switch play instantly to Spencer on the left.

No panic. No yelling. Just clean movement. Command.

Spencer drove forward with purpose and laid it off to Max down the left wing, who skipped past his marker and curled a cross into the box. It was slightly behind Adam, but Dante crashed in from the far post, forcing a rushed clearance.

Oakridge corner.

Xavier trotted over to take it. The ball in his hands was slick and damp. He placed it carefully, wiped his hands on his shorts and scanned the box.

Elijah and Aidan pushed forward. Dante stood in the middle, flanked by defenders. Adam hovered just inside the six-yard area.

Xavier raised his arm, ran up and whipped the ball to the edge of the penalty spot.

Elijah rose above his marker and nodded it goalward.

Just over the bar.

Close.

But Mountain FC no longer looked in control — their confidence was starting to crack.

Minutes ticked by. Xavier felt the rhythm of the game tilting. Oakridge was starting to control possession. Liam began to push higher, making clever runs to drag midfielders wide. Charles and Max were finding space on the flanks.

Every time Mountain tried to regain momentum, Oakridge shut it down quickly. Any long balls were intercepted. And at the centre of it all, Xavier moved like a metronome: receiving, passing, communicating.

"Back to Spencer. Time."

"Jay, hold until Charles checks in."

"Now, Max — go!"

It was starting to flow.

Then, in the 56th minute, came the moment.

Xavier received a pass near midfield, turned into space and drove forward with pace. A Mountain midfielder tried to close him down, but Xavier cut inside, then poked the ball to Liam with his left foot before getting crunched. He fell to the floor with a thud and slid on the grass, keeping his eyes on Liam.

The pass was perfect.

Liam took one touch and threaded a low through ball between the defenders.

Adam timed his run.

He was onside.

The Mountain keeper rushed out, but Adam struck it early, low and firm, across goal and into the far corner.

3–2 Oakridge.

The bench exploded. Coach Torres raised a fist. Xavier was still on the ground near midfield, holding his muddy knee in pain.

Liam was the first to help him up.

"That was amazing," Liam said.

"You finished it," Xavier replied, brushing dirt from his knee and shorts.

Adam didn't do his now-trademark faked injury celebration, as his concern for his captain was the priority after the goal, and he and the team ran over to see how Xavier was.

By that time, Xavier was gingerly on his feet with Liam turning to high-five Adam.

"Right, let's keep it tight and more of the same." Xavier knew you were most vulnerable to concede a goal right after you had scored. The next goal was crucial, he said to himself.

Mountain FC fought back hard after the goal.

They threw on extra attackers. Their right-winger nearly equalised on a break, but Lucas was quick off his line, smothering the ball with his chest. Aidan and Elijah dug deep, clearing headers and blocking shots.

Coach Torres rotated fresh legs in. Sergio replaced Liam. Ben came on for Adam. Spencer was replaced with Fabian at left back.

In the 65th minute, Oakridge nearly extended the lead when Ben beat two defenders but shot just wide.

Xavier dropped deeper to help close the game out. He and Sergio sat in a double pivot, absorbing pressure and playing simple. This set-up provided greater defensive cover and helped Oakridge build up better from the back. Coach had said it would be a mental test — and it was.

When the board went up showing four minutes of added time, Mountain FC pushed everything forward.

Xavier shouted constantly, calling out runners, shifting the shape.

"Back line — step!"

"Watch the overlap!"

"Lucas — on your right!"

The final minute. Mountain FC launched a final ball into the box. It bounced dangerously.

Elijah swung a foot and half-cleared it.

Xavier tracked back, head spinning. The ball fell to Mountain's captain near the top of the area.

He struck it hard.

Lucas dove.

It hit Aidan's thigh and deflected wide.

Corner.

The ref checked his watch.

Mountain FC brought everyone up, even their keeper came to the halfway line. Xavier scanned every player, making sure they were marking. He told Dante to push up to provide an outlet just in case they could break quickly from the corner.

The final minute, surely.

Xavier crouched near the edge of the box, heart pounding.

The ball curled in high and dangerous.

Lucas leapt into traffic and punched it clear with both fists, crashing into a crowd of bodies. The ball fell to Sergio, who had read the situation perfectly. Without hesitation, Sergio booted it long down the right-hand channel.

Dante reacted instantly.

He chased it down with a burst of speed, getting to it just before it reached the sideline. Two Mountain defenders closed in on him, one from the side, the other from behind.

Xavier had already started sprinting. He'd anticipated the clearance, breaking forward from deep. As he raced upfield through the middle, he shouted, "Take it to the corner!"

Dante hesitated. Looked up.

And saw it.

The defenders were drawn to him, doubling up, while Xavier was all alone in the centre. The keeper was retreating, backpedalling toward his area, but not yet set.

Dante took one more touch, then slid the ball inside with perfect weight.

Xavier didn't break stride.

He took one smooth first touch to settle it, just outside the box. The keeper stepped forward, arms wide, leaning slightly left.

The right side was open.

Xavier kept his cool, stayed balanced and passed the ball low into the bottom right corner with his right foot.

Time slowed.

He watched the ball roll cleanly across the grass, past the keeper's outstretched hand … and into the net.

The net rippled, and Xavier stood there for a half-second, frozen as a surge of emotion rushed through him.

Then it hit.

He had scored.

He threw both arms into the air, eyes wide, grinning so hard it hurt. The bench erupted. Liam and Spencer jumped up and down on the sidelines. Lucas pumped both fists. Coach Torres clapped with a rare flash of a smile. Sergio and Dante sprinted over to lift Xavier in the air, nearly knocking him over.

Mountain 2 Oakridge 4.

The referee barely restarted play before blowing the final whistle.

The second group match was theirs.

And Xavier, for the first time in weeks, felt something he hadn't allowed himself to feel in a while...

Joy.

Unfiltered, unstoppable joy.

The whistle blew.

Final score:

Mountain FC 2   Oakridge FC 4

Mountain 12'

Mountain 15'

                Dante 20'

                Dante 38'

                Adam 56'

                Xavier 80' +4

The team rushed the field.

Lucas was mobbed again. Xavier grinned as he jogged over to Coach Torres, who gave him a quiet nod.

"Well done," Coach said. "You kept us steady."

Xavier looked back at the group: Liam smiling shyly, Dante doing his silly dance, even Charles giving Lucas a big high-five.

For the first time in a while, Xavier didn't feel the weight.

He felt the team.

And in that moment, he knew — command didn't mean doing it alone.

It meant helping others rise with you.

Chapter 7:

Inspiration Assignment

The Monday after the Mountain FC match was anything but ordinary.

Usually, Xavier walked the school halls unnoticed. Not invisible, just quietly respected. But today, something had shifted. As he stepped through the front doors of Oakridge Middle School, the first thing he saw was a cluster of Year 7s huddled around a phone, replaying his goal from the weekend.

"I told you he was gonna score," one of them said.

"No way you called that," another replied.

Xavier gave a small nod as he passed them. They noticed. One boy even pointed and said, "That's him!" like he was some kind of celebrity.

He tried not to smile too much.

His bag felt lighter, though he hadn't taken anything out. His steps were quick, confident. Inside, he felt a strange mix of pride and pressure. The moment from Saturday — the ball leaving his boot, the net rippling, the roar of the crowd — had looped in his head all weekend. But now the glow was fading, replaced by the next challenge: staying consistent. Staying sharp. Staying worthy of the praise.

He turned the corner and spotted Liam by their lockers.

Liam was his usual calm self; hoodie up, earbuds in, flipping through a science textbook. When he saw Xavier, he gave a low-key nod.

"Morning, Captain."

Xavier chuckled. "Morning, vice-captain."

"Goal of the year," Liam said without looking up.

"Still thinking about that pass you made. Perfect weight."

Liam shrugged, but a small smile crept onto his face.

They walked together to homeroom, passing a few more congratulatory whispers and even a fist bump from one of the Year 9 boys he used to play with.

Inside Room 107, Mrs. Carter was already at her desk, sipping tea and organising a stack of papers. Dante strolled in moments later, sunglasses on, hood up, acting like he had personally lifted a trophy over the weekend.

"I've signed three notebooks and a snack wrapper already," he announced, spinning into his seat. "I'm considering charging for autographs."

"You going pro, Dante?" Xavier said, laughing.

"Er, two goals and an assist," Dante replied, leaning back. "That's like three goals."

Liam added, "So we're doing maths like that now?"

Before they could continue, Mrs. Carter stood and clapped twice.

"Alright, everyone… eyes up."

The room quieted.

"I know it's Monday. I know you're tired. And I know some of you would rather still be at the football field…" here she paused and smiled in Xavier's direction, "but we've got work to do."

A few groans, mostly playful.

"This week's assignment is about inspiration. I want you to choose someone — anyone — who inspires you. Someone who makes you want to be better. They can be from history, sports, science, your family, your neighbourhood. But your job is to tell us why they matter. What can we learn from them?"

She turned and wrote three words on the board in bold, clean strokes:

INSPIRATION. INFLUENCE. IMPACT.

"You'll write three paragraphs: one on who they are, one on what they've done, and one on why it matters to you. Add at least one quote. You'll also need a visual element. Photo, drawing, infographic, whatever fits your person. Presentations start Thursday."

A few heads dropped onto desks.

Dante raised his hand. "Can I do my cousin? He once ate thirty-six mini donuts in six minutes."

Mrs. Carter gave him the usual flat stare. "No."

Laughter rippled across the room.

She walked between the desks. "If you need help picking someone, I'll be around after class. Just remember — this is your voice. Choose someone that speaks to you."

Xavier didn't hesitate.

He turned to the margin of his notebook and scribbled a name.

Kevin De Bruyne.

There were flashier players in the world. More dramatic stories. More headlines. But De Bruyne had always been his player. Not because of the goals, though there were plenty. Not even because of the assists. It was the way he saw the game. The way he made things simple for the players around him. The way he moved without needing to dominate with words or noise.

Xavier didn't just admire De Bruyne. He wanted to play like him.

More than that, he wanted to lead like him.

After class, Xavier walked toward his next period when Mrs. Carter called his name.

"Xavier. Quick word."

He doubled back. "Yeah?"

"You've got someone in mind, don't you?"

He nodded. "Kevin De Bruyne. He's a footballer for Man City, now Napoli."

"Good choice. I don't usually get athletes. But the right one can be powerful."

Xavier smiled. "I've been watching him for years."

She tapped her pen on her notepad. "Well then, show us why."

He left the classroom with a little more purpose.

Lunchtime came with more football talk.

Lucas, Spencer, Adam and Jay all sat around their usual table. Jay was acting out the moment he almost back-heeled the ball out of bounds during a clearance gone wrong.

"Pure chaos," Adam said, laughing. "I thought Coach was going to sub you off just for the drama."

"Respect the flair," Jay said with mock pride.

Lucas turned to Xavier. "That goal's already got, like, four angles on the school's sports page. You're officially famous."

"Tell that to Dante. He won't stop messaging me clips of his assist."

"He deserves it," said Liam, biting into an apple. "Good ball."

Xavier agreed. "Everyone stepped up. That's what made the difference."

Dante joined the group and leaned across the table. "You guys talking about the last-minute goal I created? Because I had a front-row seat. It was… poetic."

"Back row," said Lucas. "Sergio gave you the perfect ball, you just had to wait and make a ten-yard pass."

"Semantics. I split those two defenders and virtually gave Xavier a tap-in," Dante said.

Xavier shook his head and laughed.

Despite the attention, despite the noise, he wasn't letting it get to him. Not this time. There was work to do, both on the field and off.

That evening, Xavier sat at his desk, laptop open, a blank Google Doc glowing on the screen.

The heading read:

Why Kevin De Bruyne Inspires Me

He stared at it for a moment, then opened a new tab and typed, "Kevin De Bruyne career highlights."

Clips flooded the screen.

He clicked on one: a pass through four defenders, perfectly timed. Another: a long-range goal struck like a laser into the top corner. But what stood out most were the interviews. Quiet. Thoughtful. Confident without showing off.

In one, De Bruyne talked about understanding teammates' movements before they made them. In another, he described how he didn't need to shout to lead; he let his decisions do the talking.

Xavier leaned back in his chair.

That was it.

That's what he was chasing.

Not just being good. Not just scoring goals. But being the kind of player others could trust because they knew he would make the right choice.

He turned back to the document and began typing.

Kevin De Bruyne isn't the loudest player on the pitch. He doesn't celebrate every goal like it's the end of the world. But he understands the game like few others do. What inspires me most is how he leads; not just with skill, but with clarity and calm under pressure. He's the kind of player who makes everyone around him better. And that's the kind of captain I want to be.

He paused and exhaled.

That felt right.

Xavier refocused, fingers flying over the keyboard as he opened up Kevin De Bruyne's Wikipedia page. He scanned the info box first:

Birthplace, Drongen, Belgium; height, 1.81 metres; position, midfielder. Then he dove into the stats. Making 422 appearances for the club, he won the UEFA Champions League, six Premier League titles, five League Cups and two FA Cups. He scribbled notes into his notebook, circling key achievements like "Premier League Player of the Season" and "Champions League Winner". He jotted down a quote De Bruyne once gave in an interview:

"I try to do the best I can to help the team, not just with goals or assists, but with movement, structure and calmness."

It was exactly what Xavier wanted to show in his presentation. Not just greatness, but why it mattered.

Xavier scrolled further down the Wikipedia page, reading about Kevin De Bruyne's early years. Born in a small town in Belgium, De Bruyne had started playing football at a young age, moving through youth academies with quiet determination. But what stood out most to Xavier was how difficult his childhood had been.

Kevin De Bruyne had faced rejection early in his career. He was once dropped from a youth team because the host family said he was "too quiet". Some coaches decided he didn't have enough personality to make it. But instead of quitting, he used it as fuel. He worked harder, moved clubs and proved every one of them wrong. Xavier underlined that part in his notes. It reminded him of Lucas — quiet, often overlooked at first, but now one of the most important players on the team. And maybe, in a different way, it reminded him of himself too.

Xavier thought about how Kevin hadn't had it easy, especially before his professional career even began. The challenges he faced weren't just about football; they were often out of his control. Yet he focused on what he could control and turned it into purpose. As Xavier stared at the screen, he began to think more deeply about his own situation and about his teammates. Some of them he only really saw at training or on match days. What was going on in their lives when they weren't wearing the Oakridge badge? What challenges were they dealing with that no one talked about? For the first time,

Xavier realised that being captain wasn't just about leading on the pitch. It was about understanding the people he led.

An hour later, his dad knocked gently and peeked in.

"Hey, dinner in ten."

"Okay."

He lingered. "Homework?"

"Yeah. Presentation for school."

"On what?"

"Someone who inspires me. I picked Kevin De Bruyne."

He smiled. "Solid choice, silky player that one. Your favourite, right?"

"Yeah."

"Well," he said, "seems like a good pick. Take your time."

He nodded, and he left.

Xavier's dad was a lifelong Manchester United fan, something Xavier had always found slightly tragic. The old red jersey still hung in the closet, and weekend mornings were often filled with grumbles about referees and stories of the glory days — Schmeichel, Van Nistelrooy, Beckham, Roy Keane.

But to his dad's mild disappointment, Xavier had fallen in love with the other side of Manchester. The sky-blue side. It wasn't rebellion, not really. It was the way City played, the beautiful passing, the movement, the control. It spoke to Xavier in a way

United's grit and grind never had. To his dad's credit, he never pushed it. When Xavier asked for a De Bruyne kit for Christmas instead of a retro Cantona one, he just smiled, shook his head and said, "Can't argue with good football."

He looked back at the screen and smiled.

Then he kept typing.

Chapter 8:

The Presentation

Thursday morning arrived faster than Xavier expected.

His presentation on Kevin De Bruyne was saved, printed and paperclipped with care. He had re-read it twice at his mum's dining table the night before, rehearsed it out loud to himself in his bedroom, and even checked the pronunciation of "Drongen" online just to be sure.

Still, as he sat at his desk in Room 107 and watched the first few classmates give their presentations, he felt a familiar flutter in his stomach.

Two students had already gone. Lena did hers on her mum, and Aidan gave a surprisingly confident speech on Dwayne "The Rock" Johnson. Mrs. Carter nodded along with each one, asking a few follow-up questions and making notes on her clipboard.

Xavier shuffled his paper a little. Liam gave him a quiet thumbs-up across the row.

Then Mrs. Carter looked up.

"Xavier? You're up."

He stood, walked to the front of the class and took a breath. He didn't mind speaking in front of the team, shouting instructions on the field or giving feedback after a match. But this was different. Everyone was quiet. Watching. Waiting.

He unfolded his notes and started.

"My presentation is on Kevin De Bruyne, a professional footballer from Belgium who played for Manchester City, now Napoli, and the Belgian national team. He's known for his passing, vision and the way he controls the tempo of the game."

A few heads perked up. Some classmates, mostly the ones who followed football, leaned in a little.

"He's won six Premier League titles, two FA Cups and was named Premier League Player of the Season. He has over 170 assists in the Premier League, which is one of the highest ever."

Xavier clicked the remote to show his printed slide: a simple page with Kevin's stats, a picture of him holding the Premier League trophy and a quote underneath.

"He once said, 'I try to do the best I can to help the team, not just with goals or assists, but with movement, structure and calmness.'"

Xavier paused and looked up. "That part stood out to me because... that's what I'm trying to do. As a midfielder and a captain, I don't just want to play well. I want to help everyone around me play better."

Mrs. Carter nodded slowly.

"He had a tough childhood. Some coaches thought he wasn't vocal enough. One host family even rejected him because they didn't like his personality. But instead of giving up, he kept going. He used the criticism to work harder, and now he's one of the best players in the world."

He paused, then glanced around the classroom.

"But instead of quitting, he kept going. He moved clubs and worked even harder. Eventually, he joined Genk, where he started playing professionally. Then he got signed by Chelsea but didn't get much playing time there. A lot of players would have disappeared after that, but he didn't. He went to Germany, proved himself at Wolfsburg, and finally made it to Manchester City, where he became one of the best midfielders in the world."

Xavier looked down at his notes and then back at the class.

Xavier held up a laminated quote he'd printed from an interview, placing it next to the visual. "He didn't need to shout to be a leader. He just understood the game better than most — and made the players around him trust him."

He looked up again.

"I chose Kevin De Bruyne because he leads in the way I want to lead. Not with noise. With clarity. Calmness. Smart decisions. And with trust."

There was a beat of silence when he finished.

Then a few classmates clapped, quietly at first, then more confidently. A couple of the football fans in the back row nodded with impressed looks.

Mrs. Carter smiled. "Thank you, Xavier. That was thoughtful and well-connected. You didn't just tell us about Kevin; you showed us why he matters to you. That's what inspiration is."

He returned to his seat, heart still pounding, but something inside felt settled. Liam gave him another nod. Dante whispered, "Goal-level presentation," and flicked a paper football through the air like a celebration.

And for the rest of the day, even during maths and science and a soggy grilled cheese at lunch, Xavier felt some pride, something solid.

Not confidence like a flash. But confidence like a foundation.

He was learning to lead.

Not just on the pitch. But everywhere.

Most of the team had already drifted toward the fence where parents waited or started gathering bags for the walk home. But Coach Torres stood still near the centre circle, arms crossed, scanning the field like he was still deep in thought. Xavier noticed.

"Xavier," Coach called, "walk with me for a minute."

Xavier adjusted the strap on his backpack and jogged over.

They moved slowly toward the centre circle. Coach stopped, toeing the line.

"You've got the tools," he said, not looking at Xavier directly. "Good touch. Sharp engine. You organise well. But if you want to lead this team deeper into the tournament, you need to see the game one pass ahead."

Xavier nodded slightly, not sure what was coming.

"I'm talking about spatial awareness and scanning," Coach continued. "You're doing some of it already, but not enough. At this level, it's the difference between being a great player and being an exceptional one."

Coach dropped a cone on the grass and pointed around the field.

"Let's say you receive the ball from Liam here. Before it even gets to you, you need to know three things: who's pressing, who's supporting and where the space is. Are you going forward, wide or recycling?"

Xavier's eyes followed Coach's pointing hand.

Coach smiled. "You can't make the best decision if you only start thinking after you've got the ball. The best midfielders in the world are always scanning. De Bruyne? Before he even receives it, he's checked his shoulder three times. He has a mental map of where everyone is. He's going to be making decisions on the next pass before it's even gotten to his foot. And that's why he looks like he has so much time, and then with his skill it's usually devastating to the opposition."

Xavier straightened up. "So, I need to scan more?"

Coach nodded. "Every five seconds. Get in the habit. Head on a swivel. Check both shoulders. Start building a picture before the ball even comes."

They walked a few more paces.

"I'm going to start tracking it in training," Coach added. "Every time you scan, I'll note it. We'll even film parts of practice next week so you can see for yourself."

Xavier grinned. "Homework on the pitch, huh?"

"Exactly," Coach said with a smirk. "You want to be our conductor? Then see the whole orchestra. Early. Always."

As they parted, Xavier jogged toward the changing room with something new in his stride. He wasn't just going to play. He was going to see the game differently.

Chapter 9:

Newport Looming

By Tuesday afternoon, the buzz from the Mountain FC win had settled and a new feeling of anticipation began to grow for the next game of the tournament.

Xavier stood near the midfield circle, watching Coach Torres set up cones in wide triangles across the pitch. The sun was out, the pitch dry and the breeze steady. Perfect conditions. Still, the atmosphere was different.

Newport Rangers were next.

The problem was — nobody really knew much about them.

Coach Torres had said as much in the team meeting earlier that day.

"They're a new team this year. I haven't seen them play. No tape. No scouting notes."

The team chuckled a little. After all, they were U13, not Manchester City. The closest thing they had to a scout was Jay's uncle, who claimed he saw a kid, probably from Newport, who nutmegged three players at a community barbecue. Spencer leaned over and whispered, "Was that before or after the hot dogs?" Everyone laughed. Even Coach cracked a small grin before shaking his head and getting back to the whiteboard.

"Alright," he said, pointing to the diagram, "even without Premier League-level intel, we prepare smart."

The room had gone quiet in anticipation for what Coach had to say. Even Dante, who usually had a comment for everything, stayed silent.

"We know their results," Coach continued. "They lost 3–0 to Mountain. Then they beat Newbridge 3–1. That tells me they're not pushovers. And it tells me they can score goals if we give them space."

"It's simple," he said, tapping the numbers. "We've got two wins, they've each got one. Newbridge are out. So, here's what happens: if we win or draw, we top the group and get home advantage in the last 16. If we lose and Mountain beats Newbridge, then all three of us will have six points, and it'll come down to goal difference."

He paused, giving the team a chance to let it sink in.

"Don't leave it to goal difference," he added, circling their name at the top. "Let's finish this clean. Let's finish it first."

Team	Played	W	D	L	For	Against	GD	Points
Oakridge FC	2	2	0	0	6	2	4	6
Mountain FC	2	1	0	1	5	4	1	3
Newport Rangers	2	1	0	1	3	4	-1	3
Newbridge United	2	0	0	2	1	5	-4	0

Group B – Game 1:

Oakridge FC 2 Newbridge United 0

Mountain FC 3 Newport Rangers 0

Group B – Game 2:

Mountain FC 2 Oakridge FC 4

Newport Rangers 3 Newbridge United 1

Group B – Game 3:

Newbridge United vs Mountain FC

Oakridge FC vs Newport Rangers

He paused, then stepped up to the whiteboard.

"So, we're going to try something new. A 4-3-3."

He drew it cleanly: four defenders, three midfielders, three attackers.

Subs: Leo, Fabian, Sergio, Ben, Ryan

"This gives us better balance and more passing options. More triangles across the pitch. That means quicker possession, more rhythm, more control."

Xavier leaned forward slightly. He liked this. It was smart and more attacking. It gave midfield more responsibility, more flexibility. It also meant he'd be at the base of a triangle, with Liam and Charles playing just ahead of him in central roles, flanked by Max and Adam wide, and Dante leading the line.

"This isn't just any formation," he said. "It's one of the most successful shapes in modern football. And some of the best managers in history have made it their blueprint."

He looked around the room, making sure they were listening.

"Pep Guardiola used the 4-3-3 to dominate with Barcelona. Busquets, Xavi and Iniesta in midfield, total control of the game.

They passed teams to death. They didn't just win; they exhausted opponents by always having an extra man in the middle."

A few of the boys nodded. Xavier already knew this part, but he still liked hearing Coach explain it. Adam turned to Xavier. "Well, if I'm on the right wing now, that makes me Messi." Xavier rolled his eyes.

"Jürgen Klopp's Liverpool used a different kind of 4-3-3. More direct, high pressing, lightning-fast transitions. With Salah and Mané out wide and Firmino dropping into pockets, they won the Champions League and Premier League playing like a pack of wolves."

Max jumped in, having overheard Dante's previous comment. "I'm the new Salah, Coach." The team giggled.

He added a quick arrow from midfield to wide attack to show how spacing worked.

"And then there's Carlo Ancelotti. He's used it everywhere — from Milan to Real Madrid — because it's flexible. You can press, you can sit back, you can dominate possession or hit on the counter. It gives you triangles all over the pitch."

Coach turned back to the team.

"Point is, this system works. But it only works if you move. If you talk. If you trust each other. No hiding. No passengers. Everyone has a role."

Xavier felt a small pulse of excitement in his chest. He already knew where he fit: at the base of the triangle. The link. The balance. The calm in the middle of it all.

"We'll work on it in training this week," Coach said. "It's not about scoring five goals. It's about keeping the ball, creating chances and staying compact when we lose it."

On the field, Xavier adjusted quickly. The new shape suited him, three passing angles instead of two, cleaner lanes to shift play left or right. He found himself checking over his shoulder more often, communicating with Aidan behind him, calling out to Dante in front.

"Man on!"

"Switch now!"

"Drop into space!"

The tempo was higher. Mistakes came faster too. Jay misread a passing lane. Charles overhit a diagonal. Even Lucas had a few awkward touches as the team tried building out from the back under pressure.

But Xavier didn't panic.

He could see the idea working. It just needed time.

After practice, he sat on the bench beside Liam, watching the sun dip behind the clubhouse.

"They're a wildcard," Liam said. "We've never seen them play."

"Coach hasn't either."

"That's rare."

"Yeah. But I think we'll be fine if we control possession. This formation makes more sense against teams we don't know."

Liam nodded, quiet as usual. But there was a question behind his eyes.

"What?" Xavier asked.

"Just thinking," Liam replied. "What if they press us the way Mountain did? We haven't practised playing out under pressure with three midfielders."

Xavier didn't answer right away. He looked out at the empty pitch. The cones were still scattered across the grass, glowing orange in the late light.

"We adapt," he finally said. "It's what we've been good at."

That night, back at his mum's condo, Xavier stood in his room, looking down at the whiteboard propped beside his desk. He'd already sketched out three or four versions of Newport's likely formation to see how Oakridge's new shape would work.

No guarantees, but he had a feeling they'd play compact and hit on the counter. If they'd beaten Newbridge but lost heavily to Mountain, they probably sat deeper against stronger teams and broke forward with pace.

He wrote three quick reminders in marker:

• *Don't force it through the middle.*

• *Play early to wide runners.*

• *Scan, scan, scan.*

Then he capped the marker, grabbed his water bottle and headed to bed.

No YouTube highlights tonight.

No diagrams.

Just rest.

Because in three days, they'd face the one thing Xavier couldn't plan for:

The unknown.

Chapter 10:

Fractures

Thursday afternoon practice started with passing triangles. Crisp, one-touch drills. Fast feet. Fast thinking. Everything Coach Torres had been hammering home all week.

"Ball never rests," he shouted as the tempo picked up. "Touch, move, touch again. Make the triangles real."

Xavier thrived in these drills. He loved the clarity. He played the pivot role with Liam to his left and Max just ahead, pinging passes between them like they were threading invisible strings. The new formation gave him space, options, flow.

But not everyone was adjusting as easily.

Charles flubbed a simple pass under pressure and immediately threw his hands up in frustration.

"Come on, man!" he shouted at Lucas, who had passed the ball to him a bit short.

"It wasn't that bad," Spencer muttered nearby.

Coach blew his whistle.

"Reset," he said calmly. "Everyone, take a breath."

They reset. The ball rolled. Xavier opened up, received the next pass from Jay and laid it off to Max in a single smooth motion.

But a few minutes later, it happened again. Charles turned the ball over during a small-sided possession game, and this time he kicked a cone across the field.

"Seriously?" he snapped. "This shape is useless if no one's moving!"

"Maybe just pass quicker," Dante fired back from the sideline. "You don't have to be angry every time."

"Alright, alright," Coach said firmly, stepping in. "Let's pause here."

The team froze. Breathing heavy. Sweat dripping. The mood was tense.

Coach Torres knelt down, picked up the cone and stood quietly for a moment before speaking.

"Listen. New shape, new system, there's going to be bumps. It's not about perfection today. It's about trust. Trusting that the guy next to you wants to win just as badly. So, before you lose your cool, ask yourself if what you're saying helps the team. Because if it doesn't, save it."

Everyone looked down.

Xavier glanced at Charles, who didn't say anything but kicked at the turf.

Coach continued as the boys took a quick water break.

"This is the right time to test this formation," he said, pointing again to the 4-3-3 on his clipboard. "Group stage isn't done yet, but we're likely through. If we want to go deep in this tournament, we need options. And this gives us more."

He tapped his marker on the midfield triangle.

"Three in the middle gives us control. It gives us triangles all over the pitch. That means fewer rushed passes, better angles and more ways out of tight spots. This won't be the last team that presses us."

Xavier watched his teammates closely. Some nodded, others still looked uncertain. Charles especially.

"And look," Coach continued, turning to face them more directly. "I've been watching training closely. Some of you are stepping up."

He turned slightly, eyes drifting toward Sergio.

"Sergio's come a long way. You've had a growth spurt or something. Taller. Stronger. His decision-making's sharper too."

A few heads turned toward Sergio, who looked slightly startled but stood a little straighter.

"I'm going to start rotating him more into the right mid position. See how he handles it."

That's when Xavier noticed the flicker in Charles's expression. Just a second. But it was there. A tight jaw. A quick glance to the grass.

From Xavier's perspective, Sergio had always been one of the quieter guys on the team. He didn't joke around like Jay, didn't flash tricks like Dante and definitely didn't talk tactics like Xavier himself. But lately something had changed. He seemed sharper. Taller, for one. Like he'd grown two inches in a month. His shoulders had filled out too, and his movement off the ball was quicker, more confident.

Xavier had noticed it during rondos. Sergio no longer played like a kid trying to keep up. Now, he anticipated the passes, cut off angles, even directed others with a quiet confidence. His touch had improved. His turns were smoother. He was starting to look like a proper midfielder.

Xavier respected it. Sergio didn't demand attention. He earned it, day by day, without the need for drama. But he also knew that kind of quiet rise could rattle someone like Charles, who had always been the automatic starter on the right. And maybe that's why Charles had looked flustered lately — like he could feel Sergio's shadow growing behind him.

Coach moved on, explaining patterns of play and movement off the ball. But the message was already delivered.

Sergio was pushing.

And Charles knew it.

Xavier filed the moment away in his mind. It helped explain why Charles had been off in training. Why he'd snapped at Lucas. Why his first touch had betrayed him more than once.

It wasn't just the new shape. It was the shift in the pecking order.

Coach Torres didn't do drama. He didn't play mind games. But he did reward performance. And Sergio had been earning it.

After training, Xavier lingered on the field to help collect cones. The sun had dipped low, casting long shadows across the grass. As he stacked the last few cones, Coach Torres walked beside him, clipboard tucked under his arm.

"Charles is frustrated," Xavier said quietly.

Coach nodded. "He's feeling the pressure. Wants to make an impact. That's not a bad thing."

"He's always been one of our best players," Xavier said. "But things are changing. Everyone's getting stronger, faster. It's different now."

Coach smiled slightly. "That's part of growing up in the game. You're all developing at different speeds, and that's where the challenge comes in. My job is to build a competitive squad. Your job is to keep adapting — keep raising your standard."

Xavier looked out across the empty field. "I just want us to play well. I think this new shape works if everyone trusts it."

Coach gave a slow nod. "That's exactly why I need you steady in the middle. You're the balance, Xavier. The link that keeps everything connected."

For a moment, neither spoke. The quiet hum of crickets filled the air. Xavier picked up the final cone and smiled.

"Got it, Coach."

Coach clapped him gently on the shoulder. "I know you do."

That night, Xavier was back at his mum's place. The TV was on in the background, but he wasn't really watching. His legs ached from training, yet his mind was still racing — the passing patterns, the movement off the ball, the body language of his teammates. Especially Charles.

He sat at the small kitchen table, a plate of leftovers beside his open laptop, when his phone buzzed.

Dante: "What's up with Charles? Looked like he was gonna throw a cone at someone today lol."

Xavier smirked, but it didn't last long.

Xavier: "Yeah. Just pressure. He'll come around."

A few seconds later, another buzz.

Dante: "You sure? He's not talking to anyone in the group chat."

Xavier stared at the screen. Charles could be hot-headed sometimes, but lately he seemed frustrated a lot of the time. He wasn't joking around like usual.

Xavier: "I'll talk to him. Maybe his brother knows something?"

He set the phone down and leaned back in his chair. The house was still, the faint hum of the fridge filling the silence.

This was the part of being captain no one ever mentioned — the quiet part, the invisible work. The glue that held things together when emotions started to fray. He couldn't just assume Charles was upset because of football. Maybe it wasn't the new formation, or Sergio getting more minutes. Maybe something was going on at school, or at home with Jay.

Xavier looked at his phone again, the group chat still open, the unread messages piling up.

He knew what he had to do. Tomorrow, he'd pull Charles aside — not as captain giving orders, but as a friend who cared enough to ask.

Friday arrived with a sharper edge in the air. Last practice before the game. Coach kept it light: passing drills, small-sided games and set pieces.

Afterward, Xavier caught up with Charles.

"Hey," he said casually, handing him a water bottle. "You alright?"

Charles hesitated, then nodded slowly. "Just… feel like I'm not doing enough. In this new shape, I'm not on the ball as much, and when I am, I seem to make the wrong decision."

"You don't need touches to make an impact," Xavier said. "Your movement pulls defenders. Your pressure forces mistakes. You're still key."

Charles gave a weak smile. "Coach say that?"

"No," Xavier replied. "I did."

And with that, Charles gave him a quick fist bump before jogging off.

The storm, for now, had passed.

Chapter 11:

Formation Test

Saturday morning arrived with overcast skies and a low fog hanging above the turf. Oakridge's home field wasn't flashy, but they loved it. The pitch sat snug inside a tall chain-link fence that wrapped around its edges, keeping the crowd just far enough back. It gave the coaches room to spread out: cones lined the touchline, pinnies hung off goalposts, and the oversized ball bags sat open near the bench, safely out of the way. The fence kept things contained but never quiet; the sound of cleats striking turf, voices calling out instructions and parents cheering carried freely through the open air.

Around the pitch ran an old rubber track, worn smooth but still well kept. In the mornings, it belonged to the slow walkers — mostly older folks in track pants and sneakers, moving at a gentle pace, chatting about the weather or the news. They rarely paid attention to the football, but their steady presence gave the place a sense of life, like the field was never really empty.

Evenings, though, were different. Families gathered along the fence line, some standing, others sitting in folding chairs with coolers and coffee cups nearby. Most leaned on the fence, calling out encouragement or murmuring about tactics like sideline analysts. A few parents wandered the track, walking the same loop over and over, following the game from different angles as if quietly coaching from the shadows.

Beyond the far goal on the south side sat a small public park. The swings creaked, the metal slide gleamed from years of use, and laughter from the younger siblings filled the air. They climbed and played, occasionally glancing toward the field to catch a glimpse of their brothers in action.

It wasn't a stadium. But for the boys of Oakridge, it felt like something better — their home, their patch of grass, their field of dreams.

Xavier got out of his mum's car, his boots in hand, hood up and headphones in. His game-day playlist was soft today, mostly instrumental stuff. Calm. Rhythmic. Like the passing triangles Coach had drilled all week.

In the distance, the Newport Rangers players were already warming up. They looked sharp in teal kits with white trim. Xavier scanned them carefully. Their movements were crisp. Focused. They didn't look like a team that had lost 3–0 to Mountain FC.

"Unknown quantity," Coach Torres had said in the pre-game talk. "No tape. No history. But they're here, and they earned it. We respect that."

Xavier nodded to himself and entered the changing room.

In the changing room, Coach stood in front of the line-up, already written out on the whiteboard.

"Sergio, you've been playing great all week, although you'll start on the bench... be ready, you'll come in second half," Coach said. "We'll see how they handle pace on the right wing. But we start with what's worked."

He turned to the midfield triangle and pointed at each name.

"Xavier, sit and screen. Keep our tempo. Liam, Charles — rotate forward. Make late runs. Don't lose shape."

Then to the front three.

"Adam, hug the touchline, force their left back wide. Max, cut inside when Spencer overlaps. Dante — be the pivot. Hold it up."

Coach drew a triangle between Xavier, Liam and Charles.

"Control the midfield, and we win the match."

The game began in a blur. Newport Rangers were better than expected — fast, compact and organised. They didn't press high, but they didn't sit deep either. Instead, they swarmed the ball whenever Oakridge crossed midfield.

Xavier felt it immediately. The spaces were tighter. The angles closed faster.

In the 10th minute, Newport's striker nearly broke through on a long ball over the top, but Lucas was quick off his line to scoop it up.

"Wake up!" Xavier shouted, already scanning for options. "We're too flat!"

The new shape was holding, for now, but Charles wasn't getting much of the ball. His runs were too wide, being used to playing more on the wing, which exposed Xavier and Liam. And after one miscontrolled pass, he stomped the turf in frustration.

Xavier jogged over.

"Tuck in a little. Give your brother Jay space to overlap."

Charles didn't say anything, just nodded curtly.

By the 18th minute, Oakridge had settled slightly. The midfield triangle began to find rhythm. Xavier dropped deep to receive from Elijah, then played a sharp one-two with Liam before threading it to Max, who turned into space. There was a much bigger attacking threat now with three forwards.

It didn't lead to a shot, but it was a sign: the 4-3-3 was working, if they kept faith in it.

The breakthrough came in the 26th minute.

97

Dante received a switch from Spencer, cut inside and drove forward. Max and Adam made their runs, which drew away the defenders. Dante continued forward and, with defenders backing off, he curled a left-footed ball low and hard just inside the post. The keeper got a hand to it but couldn't stop it.

1–0. Oakridge.

The bench erupted. Dante's goal celebrations always had flair, but this one had extra swagger.

As the ball rippled the net, he wheeled away from the box with a grin that stretched from ear to ear. He didn't sprint or slide — he strutted. Shoulders loose, chest out, one hand pointing casually to the sky. Then, with a slow turn back toward the crowd, he raised his right index finger and wagged it side to side, eyes locked on the sideline like he was saying, "You should've known."

It was pure Dante: confident, playful and just a little theatrical. His teammates mobbed him before he could milk it any further, but not before a few parents chuckled from behind the fence.

"He's been practising that in the mirror," Adam muttered, laughing as he jogged over.

Coach clapped once, then called Xavier over.

"They'll come at us now. Make sure Liam drops when we lose it. We can't leave you isolated."

Xavier nodded and jogged back, relaying the instructions.

Newport did push forward. Their central midfielder, a stocky number 8, began dictating play, spraying passes wide, testing Oakridge's fullbacks.

In the 34th minute, they got their reward. A quick one-two down the right caught Spencer out of position. A low cross zipped through the box. Their striker timed it perfectly and tapped it in at the far post.

1–1.

Xavier clenched his jaw but didn't panic. He turned to Liam. "We tighten up. Reset the shape. Don't dive in."

Jay and Charles had always had that unspoken brother connection on the pitch, the kind of instinctive link that didn't need words. Jay, solid and composed at right back, knew exactly when Charles was about to make a run down the wing. And Charles, explosive and eager, trusted Jay to find him in stride with those crisp diagonal passes. They worked the flank well, exchanging quick one-twos, drawing defenders out of shape.

But with Charles staying more centrally in the 4-3-3, Jay's balls were bypassing Charles up to Adam. When Charles did get the ball, he looked a little lost. The touchline was far away, and he had so many options compared to right wing. His distribution with the ball just wasn't quick enough, getting caught often or not reading the runs from the front three. Through balls sailed too deep, or cutbacks were a step behind. Jay clapped his hands encouragingly after each

100

one, but the frustration showed in Charles's eyes. The connection was there. It just needed time to adjust.

Just before halftime, Charles lost the ball again. His touch was off, and he wasn't tracking back quickly. Coach didn't yell, but he made the sub early.

"Sergio," he called. "Right side of centre midfield. Now."

Charles walked off, head down, and sat quietly on the bench.

Sergio entered with a burst of energy, immediately pressing hard and putting in a strong tackle. He fed the ball inside to Dante, who carried the ball forward.

Sergio and Dante had started to build an unexpected chemistry on the pitch. Sergio, usually more reserved, had found a rhythm with Dante's bold, aggressive style. In one play, Sergio picked up the ball near midfield and calmly slipped it between two defenders with a perfectly weighted pass. Dante, already on the move, darted onto it like he'd read Sergio's mind. Without breaking stride, he flicked it forward, shielded off a challenge and laid it back for Sergio with the outside of his boot. It was smooth. Sharp. Like two players speaking the same language — one fluent in control, the other in chaos. Together, they made it work.

The half ended evenly. 1–1.

Back in the changing room, Coach kept it composed.

"We've had control for long stretches. Keep using the triangles. Move the ball quickly. No hero passes."

He looked directly at Xavier.

"Keep us calm. Control their playmaker. And remember, they need the win more than we do. That gives us the edge."

Xavier took a deep breath.

He was ready.

Chapter 12:

Unfamiliar Faces

The second half began like a chess match, tight and controlled, each team searching for the smallest opening. For the first fifteen minutes, Oakridge looked sharper. The 4-3-3 was flowing now, the triangles forming and shifting just as Coach Torres had drilled. Xavier stayed central, scanning constantly, checking over his shoulder every few seconds the way Coach had taught him. He could see the whole field that way: the movement of his teammates, the positioning of defenders, the space about to open before it even existed.

It started with Elijah stepping in to intercept a lazy pass from Newport's midfield. He cushioned it perfectly to Liam, who took one touch before sliding it wide to Adam on the right. Adam held up play, back to goal, waiting for support. Two defenders pressed in, but Adam's balance held firm. He glanced over his shoulder once, then twice, and saw Xavier making his run through the middle.

"Go on, Xav!" Dante called, his voice echoing from the left.

Adam didn't hesitate. He shifted the ball onto his right foot and slipped a precise pass between the two centre backs. Xavier had already read it — he'd seen it coming before Adam even turned. That extra half-second from scanning the field made all the difference.

He met the pass in stride, one perfect touch to control it forward, his eyes flicking up just long enough to see the keeper rushing off his line. Calm and focused, Xavier opened his body and guided the ball with the inside of his right foot toward the far post.

One bounce. Then the net rippled with that sweet, satisfying sound.

Xavier smiled as the ball settled in the corner, his heartbeat steady, his breath calm. The moment felt effortless, like the game had slowed down just for him. Then Dante was the first to reach him, leaping onto his back with a laugh, followed by Liam and Adam, grinning wide.

Even Coach Torres clapped from the sideline, his arms folded but his eyes proud.

That goal wasn't luck. It was awareness, trust and timing — the kind of moment that made Xavier feel like he was finally playing the game the way it was meant to be played.

2–1 Oakridge.

The players roared. Sergio ran over, screaming. Lucas raised both gloves in triumph from across the pitch.

Xavier could see both his parents in the crowd; they were standing together, cheering for him.

Coach Torres applauded from the sideline and glanced at his watch.

"Ref, how much time left?" Xavier said.

"Twenty-one minutes to play," the ref said.

Coach Torres turned to the bench. "Let's make some changes, close this out."

In the 60th minute, Coach called for subs.

"Xavier, off. Ryan, you're in midfield. Liam — anchor role. Sergio right. Ryan left. Let's stay compact."

Xavier blinked. "You sure, Coach? There's still time…"

"We've got it," Coach said, firm. "You did your job. Take a well-earned rest."

Xavier jogged off reluctantly. Jay came off next for Fabian, and Dante made way for Leo.

The team was winning, but lots of changes in key areas were a worry for Xavier: Liam in the holding role, flanked by two substitutes, neither known for midfield control. Charles glanced towards Jay on the sideline, brow furrowed.

The extra energy on the field, though, seemed to make up for it. Coach Torres said to Xavier, "We need to try players in case you or others get injured." This made sense, but a big change all at once with a new formation was risky.

"Fabian's drifting inside too much," Jay said under his breath. "Spencer's getting isolated."

Charles nodded, his arms crossed. "And Ryan's not tracking back. Look at that space between Liam and the back line…"

But their words were drowned out by Coach shouting instructions, trying to keep the midfield stitched together. The subs gave some new energy, and the momentum was all in Oakridge's favour.

It didn't last.

In the 66th minute, Newport regained possession after a lazy square pass between Ryan and Liam. The ball popped loose, and their midfielder pounced. No one stepped up. He took a touch and — bang.

A thunderbolt from thirty yards out.

Lucas leapt, but it was unstoppable.

2–2.

From the sideline, Xavier stood up, cupping his hands to his mouth. "Liam! Stay central! Ryan, tuck in!"

Coach barked over him. "Settle! Make sure we close down quickly and stop long shots."

It was against the run of play. Newport had looked out of it. But the belief had shifted. Newport smelt blood.

Coach Torres paced the sideline, arms crossed tightly, eyes scanning the pitch. The 4-3-3, so fluid in training, was starting to crumble under pressure and lack of familiarity. Newport had seized the momentum, and the midfield trio, reshuffled after the substitutions, looked unsure of their roles. Ryan drifted too wide, Sergio was stepping too high, and Liam was stretched trying to plug every gap alone. Coach could see the confusion: hesitations in movement, glances over shoulders, players second-guessing. It wasn't working.

With ten minutes left and the score still level, he made the call. He signalled to Ben and pointed toward Max, switching things back to a familiar 4-4-2. It wasn't about risk anymore. It was about damage control. Two solid lines, restore the structure, give the boys something they knew. Maybe that would be enough.

Oakridge dropped into a 4-4-2, hoping to weather the last storm.

It only made things worse.

With Liam overworked in the middle and no true link-up from back to front, Oakridge resorted to long clearances. They couldn't hold the ball. Newport kept coming.

Jay and Charles were pacing now.

"They're sitting too deep," Charles muttered. "We've got no outlet."

Xavier stood near the bench, half watching the game, half running numbers in his head. At 2–2, Oakridge were still top of the group. A draw meant seven points. Enough to finish first, enough to earn home advantage in the next round. Mountain had already beaten Newport and lost to Oakridge, sitting on three points. Newport would be on four if this result held. He exhaled slowly.

A draw gets us through in first. Just don't lose.

But even as he thought it, he could feel the control slipping. Newport looked hungry, energised by their equaliser. The midfield was out of rhythm, the subs still adjusting. He glanced at the clock. Four minutes to go. The maths said "play it safe". But the momentum on the field said otherwise.

Then… heartbreak.

A scramble down the right, a missed interception by Fabian, and a low cross deflected up off Aidan's shin. It looped perfectly to Newport's striker near the penalty spot.

He volleyed it into the top corner.

3–2 Newport.

Three minutes to go.

Xavier crouched on the sideline, fists balled into the grass. "Come on. Press. Press together!"

But the energy had drained. The clock ticked down. Oakridge pushed forward in desperation, but Newport cleared everything. Lucas tried one last long kick, but it bounced harmlessly out for a throw-in.

The final whistle blew.

Coach Torres stared at the ground. A few Oakridge players sank to their knees. Elijah punched the air in frustration. Liam just stood there, frozen, looking to the bench where Xavier sat, silent and seething.

In the post-match huddle, Coach Torres gathered the boys near the halfway line. No one said a word. The sound of parents clapping politely from the fence faded into the background.

Coach didn't yell. He didn't need to.

"We didn't close it out," he began, his voice calm but firm. "That one's on me. I made too many changes too early, thinking we had the game wrapped up. That's football. You think you're in control, and in a blink, it turns."

A few of the boys stared down at their cleats. No one wanted to make eye contact.

Coach continued, "But listen — this doesn't erase what you've done so far. We've made it out of the group stage. That's a huge step. We're into the knockouts, and that means new energy, new opportunity."

He looked around the circle, making sure every player heard him. "I made those subs because I wanted to give everyone a chance to play in this formation before the next round. I wanted to see how we'd adapt when things changed. And now we know what happens when we lose our shape. These are lessons you only get by living through them."

Xavier lifted his head slightly, catching Coach's eye.

Torres nodded at him. "You held the middle well today. We'll talk Monday. There's work to do, but it's good work."

A few players shuffled, shoulders relaxing just a little.

Coach's voice softened. "Don't hang your heads. You earned your spot in the next round. Not every team gets that. Now we regroup, we recover and we move forward. Knockout football is a whole new story."

He gave a small smile and clapped his hands once. "Proud of you, boys. Now go shake hands, heads high."

The boys broke from the huddle, still disappointed but walking a little taller. The sting of the loss was there, but so was something else, a spark of excitement for what came next.

Final Score:

Oakridge FC 2   Newport Rangers 3

Dante 26'

              Newport 34'

Xavier 58'

              Newport 66'

              Newport 77'

Chapter 13:

Reset

Training was quiet on Monday.

Not silent, cleats still echoed on concrete, balls still thudded against the fence, but the usual buzz was gone. No playful banter between warm-ups. No one showing off flicks or crossbar challenges. Just focused, clipped touches and players looking at the ground a little more than usual.

Xavier arrived early, headphones in, hoodie pulled low. He'd spent most of Sunday replaying the match in his head. The goal he'd scored felt distant now, muted by the frustration of sitting on the sideline as it all slipped away.

Coach Torres didn't speak much during the first twenty minutes. Just observed. He let them go through their passing patterns and rondos without interruption. No corrections. No praise. Just presence.

Finally, he called them into a huddle.

"Alright," Coach said. "Let's talk."

Everyone gathered. Lucas at the back, arms crossed. Dante still had his hands tucked into his sleeves. Jay stood beside Charles. Xavier dropped to one knee.

"I'm not going to pretend that Saturday didn't sting," Coach started. "We had that match. Then we lost it. That happens in football, especially at this level. We need to be able to respond better to changes in games."

A few players looked at the grass. Charles fiddled with the edge of his sock.

"But here's the bigger picture. We're through. Not first in the group, no. That's the price of letting a game slip. Mountain had won 4–0 and topped the group on goal difference. But we're in the last sixteen. And now it's win or go home."

Team	Played	W	D	L	For	Against	GD	Points
Mountain FC	3	2	0	1	9	4	5	6
Oakridge FC	3	2	0	1	8	5	3	6
Newport Rangers	3	2	0	1	6	6	0	6
Newbridge United	3	0	0	3	1	9	-8	0

Mountain FC 4 Newbridge United 0

Oakridge 2 Newport Rangers 3

He paused.

"That means we reset."

He looked around the circle, letting the silence do the work.

"We're going to work hard this week. Not to punish ourselves. But to prepare. The knockout stage is a different beast. We need discipline, we need focus, and most of all… we need trust."

He pointed to the whiteboard behind him, now propped against the fence.

"Every player matters. Every minute counts. And that includes the moments on the bench, in warm-ups, or shouting instructions from the sideline."

Xavier felt that one in his chest.

Coach glanced at him briefly, then at Liam, then at Charles.

"We're going to train different combinations this week. We're going to clean up communication. We're going to tighten our shape."

He turned to Dante and Sergio.

"And up top, I want more connection. Sergio, your first touch and passing has improved. Dante, your finishing has been sharp. But we need to link up. One goal isn't enough anymore."

Sergio gave a small nod. Dante raised his eyebrows but didn't argue.

Then Coach looked toward the centre backs.

"Elijah. Aidan. Talk more. Loud and early. Especially on set pieces. And Jay, help Fabian find the right positioning when he's on. You're experienced now. Use it."

Jay gave a quiet "got it."

Coach clapped his hands once.

"Alright. No sulking. No blame. Let's earn our momentum back."

"I think the group stage fixtures will come out on Wednesday."

The players jogged back into drills with a little more energy.

As Xavier lined up for a possession game, he caught Coach's eye. Torres gave him a slight nod, the kind that said, *your time's not over. Be ready.*

Xavier nodded back.

It was time to reset.

Later that day, the mood was a little different at school.

At lunchtime, the playground was buzzing. A football pinged between feet on the basketball court, and scattered groups of boys huddled around picnic tables, all talking about the same thing: the knockout rounds.

Xavier walked out with his sandwich in hand, scanning for a quiet spot. But he spotted Lucas already sitting on the low concrete wall near the climbing frame with Noah next to him.

Noah had a bright red Hartford FC hoodie on over his uniform. He waved Xavier over.

"Yo, Xav! You see the draw's coming out tonight?" Noah grinned, unwrapping a granola bar.

Xavier nodded. "Yeah, can't wait to see who we get."

Noah leaned forward, elbows on his knees. "You guys finished top in your group, right?"

Xavier shook his head. "Nah. Second place, on goal difference."

Noah raised an eyebrow. "Tough one. We finished second too. But we smacked our last group game. I got two goals."

Lucas smiled. "He's being humble. One of them was a volley top corner."

"Half volley," Noah corrected with a mock grin. "But yeah, it was sweet."

The three of them sat in silence for a moment, listening to a chorus of kids yelling across the court. Someone tried a bicycle kick and landed on their back. Groans and laughter followed.

"So, we could draw each other," Noah said, breaking the quiet.

"Us vs. Hartford?" Xavier said, raising an eyebrow. "That'd be something."

Lucas chuckled nervously. "Not sure I want to face shots from you, Noah! I know your power!"

Noah laughed. "You know all my moves, Lucas, and I'd still have to get past you first, Cap. But hey, whoever we get, bring it on. Knockout round's different. You can't coast anymore. Hopefully we meet in the final."

Xavier nodded. "Yeah. One game at a time. No safety net."

They sat there for a bit longer, chewing, chatting, half-joking about wild matchups and dream goals. But beneath it all, the tension was real. Every team left was serious. Every game was everything now.

And none of them wanted their tournament to end early.

Chapter 14:

Sand and Sunlight

The sun was already warming the streets when Xavier wheeled his bike into the park, his backpack bouncing lightly on his back. Dante was already there, sitting on a bench with one leg slung over the handlebars of his own beat-up mountain bike, chewing on the end of an energy bar.

"You're late," Dante called as Xavier rolled up beside him.

"I'm two minutes early."

"Exactly. Late for being early."

Liam arrived a few minutes later, coasting in with his usual quiet energy and a Bluetooth speaker clipped to his backpack, playing a mellow beat. With their towels, a ball and a couple of water bottles in tow, they pedalled the final stretch together. Up past the bluff, through the coastal trail and finally down the ramp that led straight onto the beach.

It wasn't crowded yet. Just a few joggers near the surf and a couple of families setting up umbrellas. The tide was out, leaving a wide expanse of damp, smooth sand perfect for football or flopping around doing nothing.

They found a spot just past the lifeguard tower and threw their towels down. Shoes came off instantly, toes dug into warm sand and backpacks dropped with a thud.

"This," Dante declared, "is peak performance."

For the first while, they just soaked it in.

Liam lay on his back, arms spread wide like a starfish. Xavier kicked at a stick buried in the sand. Dante adjusted the angle of his towel three times, trying to get the best sun. He lay back with his hands behind his head, like some kind of beach king.

"Alright," Dante said suddenly, popping up and brushing sand off his chest. "I need a workout."

"Aren't we resting?" Xavier said, eyes closed behind his sunglasses.

"I've got an idea. Let's bury ourselves. Up to the knees. I need some resistance for my abs."

"You're not serious," Liam said.

But of course, he was.

They each dug a little trench, more for fun than structure, and took turns sitting in, legs covered in a mound of soft sand. Dante started doing exaggerated crunches, groaning like a gym rat.

"Beach gains," he muttered. "Feel the burn."

"More like feel the sand rash," Liam said.

Then it became headers.

Still stuck waist-deep, they tried to lean and nod the ball at each other. Liam threw soft lobs that landed nowhere near their heads, often bouncing off their chests or shoulders.

"This is not going to plan," Xavier said, laughing as the ball smacked into his collarbone.

Dante tried to rock back and forth, managing one pathetic flinch before falling sideways into the sand. They all burst out laughing.

It was dumb. It was perfect.

Later, they cooled off in the shallows, wading up to their knees and skipping stones out over the waves. Dante bragged about his nine-skip record. Liam tried to beat it but only managed six.

They dried off, grabbed slushies from the kiosk and sat on the lifeguard ramp for a bit, letting the ocean breeze dry their hair.

That's when they saw them, three boys juggling a ball near the dune line. One had a bright yellow top and impeccable control. Another was barefoot but pulling off tricks effortlessly. The third juggled side-footed, arms wide for balance.

"Game?" Dante asked.

Xavier didn't need convincing.

A few minutes later, they'd introduced themselves. The three boys were from Green Valley, a team Xavier remembered playing last season. A smart team. He asked them if they were in the tournament. They were, unbeaten in their group.

"Three-on-three?" one asked.

"First to five," Xavier said, grinning.

They cleared a patch of sand between two big pieces of driftwood. No real goals, just shirts on top of sticks they found close by.

The game was chaos in the best way. The sand made everything harder and funnier. Simple turns became stumbles. Chips and backheels were all part of the show.

Dante, as always, went full flair: rainbows, flicks, even an attempted scissor-kick that sent him spinning into the sand. Liam played solidly, tracking runs and making smart passes. Xavier stayed composed, directing traffic and feeding through balls in the little gaps.

The Green Valley kids were slick too. One of them nutmegged Dante and grinned. Another went for a dummy that actually worked. It was free-flowing and fast, even on tired legs.

One of the best plays came when Xavier backheeled a pass to Liam, who floated a soft chip across the sand. Dante met it mid-step, side-footing it past the hoodie goalpost.

"BOOM!" Dante shouted, pumping his fist and wagging his finger like he'd just scored at Wembley.

They didn't keep a real score after a while. It wasn't the point.

When the sun started dropping toward the water, the two groups shook hands, said good luck and drifted off in separate directions.

Back on their towels, the Oakridge trio lay still for a few minutes, silent except for the sound of waves and the occasional bark from the dog park up the hill.

"I vote beach day once a week," Dante mumbled, eyes closed.

"You'd be too sunburnt to play," Liam said.

"I'd still look good doing it."

Xavier chuckled and took a long drink of water.

For the first time in a while, he wasn't thinking about formations or opponents or what Coach might say at training.

They dropped their bikes lazily against the side of Dante's house. His place was just a few blocks off the main strip. A modest single-storey home with faded green shutters and a wide front porch that creaked when you stepped on it. There was a half-deflated football sitting in the garden bed and two scooters leaning by the door that probably hadn't been used in a year.

Inside, the smell of pizza was already in the air.

"Boys!" Dante's mum called from the kitchen, waving a greasy pizza box like a trophy. "Two pepperoni, one Hawaiian, and a whole lotta napkins."

Dante's dad was at the kitchen counter cutting slices with a sharp pizza wheel, like he always did. "Hungry?" he asked, already knowing the answer.

"Starving," Xavier said.

"Destroyed on the beach," Liam added with a tired smile.

The three of them plopped down at the dining table, loading up paper plates while Dante's parents hovered and chatted. They always had music playing, some old reggae or R&B, and were the type to ask about school and actually listen to the answer.

Xavier liked coming here. It felt warm and homely.

Liam didn't talk as much, but he was always paying attention. His blonde hair was parted in the middle, and he wore a faded Canada football hoodie practically every day. He was lean but strong, with a quiet confidence that showed in how he passed and moved rather than how he spoke. On the field, he was all balance and control, the kind of player who made others around him look better.

Off the field, Liam mostly kept to himself, but around Xavier and Dante he loosened up a little. Enough to toss in a sarcastic comment or a smirk when Dante got too loud.

Which was often.

After pizza, they sprawled on beanbags in Dante's room, a cluttered space with jerseys on the walls and old cleats piled in the corner. The TV flickered with the loading screen of EA Sports FC.

"2v1," Liam said, already grabbing a controller. "Me and Xavier versus Dante."

Dante stood dramatically. "That's not even fair to you guys."

"You're Southampton," Xavier said.

"What? You want to be humiliated?" said Dante.

"Bring it," Liam said, tightening his grip on the controller.

Grumbling, Dante selected his underdog squad while Liam picked Barcelona. They dove into match after match, the three of them shouting, laughing and leaning into each other as the goals poured in.

Xavier and Liam made a good team: calm possession, clever through balls, coordinated runs. Dante, naturally, went full flair again, long shots from midfield, roulette turns in his own box, and yelling "MESSI!" every time he cut inside with a left-footed winger.

After one particularly wild comeback win, Dante threw his controller in the air and flopped backwards onto the carpet.

"I'm cooked," he said. "Beach ball. Pizza. Humiliation. I need a nap."

Xavier laughed and leaned back against the bed.

Tomorrow they'd be back to training. Back to tactics and formations and the pressure of the knockout round.

But tonight? It was just three boys, full of pizza and sand, playing football in pixels and memories.

Chapter 15:

The Draw

The cafeteria at school was unusually loud for a Tuesday. Trays clattered, chairs scraped, and the air buzzed with chatter, but at one particular table near the windows, the only noise was the impatient tapping of fingers on a phone screen.

Xavier, Dante and Liam hovered around Dante's phone, refreshing the regional tournament site every thirty seconds.

"They said noon, after they didn't release anything last night," Dante muttered.

"It's noon," Liam replied calmly.

"Then where's the draw?"

Xavier didn't respond. He was too focused, his thumb swiping down the screen once more. And then finally the bracket appeared.

He leaned in, reading through the match-ups.

"There," he said, pointing at the first entry on the list. "Eastshore Rovers vs. Oakridge FC."

"They topped their group, right?" asked Liam.

"Yeah, they must have," Xavier said. "Three wins. Didn't concede a goal. That's serious."

Dante grinned. "So are we."

That afternoon, the Oakridge players gathered around Coach Torres just off the halfway line at their home pitch. The fence around the field kept parents leaning in from a distance, but within the circle it was just the boys and the coach, and a stack of white cones and a bag of balls at his feet.

Coach had a dry-erase board in hand.

"I want to try something different," he said. "Then we'll talk about the draw."

He turned the board around and showed a 4-3-3 formation.

"Three in midfield gives us more control," he explained. "We create triangles all over the field. It's great when we want to dominate possession, especially when teams press."

He paused, scanning the faces. Most looked intrigued. Some, like Charles, seemed uncertain.

"But with 4-3-3," he continued, "our wide players have to defend more. Midfield spacing has to be tight. If we lose the ball high up the pitch, there are gaps and teams like Eastshore will punish that."

He erased and redrew a 4-4-2.

"This is our base. Two banks of four. More compact. Easier to recover shape. I want us comfortable in both. Sometimes we'll start one way and switch mid-game. That's how good teams win tournaments, with options."

Jay and Charles stood side by side, heads tilted slightly toward each other, eyes on the board. Xavier saw the gears turning. They were the flank pairing who'd need to adjust most between systems.

Training that day was sharp. Lucas stood in goal, gloves adjusted, eyes moving constantly. As the team ran through drills with both shapes, he noticed the subtle changes.

With the 4-3-3, Oakridge looked more dangerous going forward, but the shape came with risks. They would be more vulnerable to counterattacks and the fullbacks were left exposed whenever they pushed up. The system demanded constant movement and high work rates, especially from the wingers and holding midfielder.

By contrast, the 4-4-2 felt steadier. The spacing was cleaner, the roles simpler. Lucas could play longer goal kicks without hesitation, knowing Dante and Adam were ready to challenge for second balls. It might not have offered the same midfield control, but it gave Oakridge better balance and fewer gaps to exploit, especially against counterattacks down the flanks.

Coach Torres clapped his hands for attention. "Alright boys… listen up."

The chatter quieted. The team leaned forward, sweaty and tired after practice but suddenly buzzing with curiosity. Xavier noticed even Dante stopped juggling a spare ball. Coach walked to the whiteboard and flipped it around, revealing a freshly drawn tournament bracket.

"Here's the official knockout draw," he said, tapping the top left corner. "We're in."

Then he read it out slowly, writing each pair in marker as he went:

♛ U13 TOURNAMENT – ROUND OF 16

Oakridge FC	vs	Eastshore Rovers
Green Valley	vs	Pinecrest United
Hartford FC	vs	Lakeside Wolves
Northbridge FC	vs	Westhill Storm
Willow Creek	vs	Riverway FC
Brookside FC	vs	Ashwood Juniors
Ironwood Athletic	vs	Copper City
Mountain FC	vs	Verwood FC

Murmurs filled the locker room.

"Verwood's tough," Jay whispered.

"Where even is Copper City?" Charles said, tilting his head.

Coach pointed to the full bracket now displayed across the board, arrows and boxes tracing the path from the Round of 16 to the final.

"We're top left," he said. "If we win our match against Eastshore, we'll play the winner of Green Valley and Pinecrest. So, start imagining that pathway."

He turned to Lucas. "Looks like Hartford are also on our side. Noah's team. We wouldn't meet them unless both reached the semi-finals."

That got a few smiles and a few raised eyebrows.

"Every match from here on is do-or-die," Coach said. "There are no second chances. This is where things get real."

Round of 16	Quarter Finals	Semi Finals	Final
Eastshore Rovers Oakridge FC	Winner Match 1 vs Winner Match 2	Winner QF1	
GreenValley Pinecrest United		Vs	
Hartford FC Lakeside Juniors	Winner Match 3 vs Winner Match 4	Winner QF2	
Northbridge FC Westhill Storm			Winner SF1 vs Winner SF2
WillowCreek Riverway FC	Winner Match 5 vs Winner Match 6	Winner QF3	
Brookside FC Ashwood Wolves		Vs	
Ironwood Athletic Copper City	Winner Match 7 vs Winner Match 8	Winner QF4	
Mountain FC Verwood FC			

Xavier stared at the bracket. His eyes locked on the Oakridge name, then followed the invisible path forward. Eastshore first. Then maybe Green Valley. Then... who knew?

It was tournament time.

After training, as the sun dipped low over the fence and parents started collecting gear from the sideline, Lucas lingered by his bag and pulled out his phone.

He checked the bracket again.

Hartford FC had drawn Lakeside Juniors in the round of 16. If both Oakridge and Hartford kept winning, they'd meet in the semi-finals.

Lucas exhaled slowly. That meant facing Noah. His old teammate. His best friend.

And just above that? Green Valley.

"They're in our quarter," he muttered.

Green Valley was no joke. Xavier, Dante and Liam had played with a few of their players on the beach. They were good, skilled. A striker who scored five in one group game. They'd be a serious test if Oakridge made it to the quarters.

"Focus on Eastshore first," Coach had said. "One game at a time."

But it was hard not to look ahead.

Back in the changing room, Coach walked in with his clipboard tucked under one arm.

"You've all seen the bracket," he said. "I'm not going to pretend it's easy. Every team left has earned their spot. But we belong here too."

He pointed to a sheet on the wall, the full tournament tree.

"We win this weekend, we move forward. One step at a time. Don't think about Green Valley. Don't think about semi-finals. Just Eastshore."

He turned to Xavier.

"You're our balance in the middle. Help the team shift between shapes. If we start 4-4-2 and need to change, you're the first voice I want them to hear."

Xavier nodded.

As the team left the changing room, the buzz was electric; excitement, nerves and quiet focus blended in the air like static. Xavier stayed behind for a moment, standing in front of the now-familiar whiteboard, eyes tracing the lines that led from Oakridge FC to the final.

His fingers gently tapped the spot where their name was written.

He thought back to his school presentation. Kevin De Bruyne's calm brilliance on the pitch. The way he saw the game two steps ahead, made space where none existed and let his play do the talking. There was one quote Xavier had found during his research, scribbled into the corner of his notebook:

"I don't care about being the best player. I care about making my team better."

That stuck with him. He wasn't chasing trophies for himself. He just wanted to lead right. To help his teammates rise.

Then came another memory: how his dad talked with a passion about Roy Keane's leadership.

"You don't need to be loud to be a leader. But when it's time to speak, speak with purpose. And when it's time to act, don't hesitate."

Simple. Sharp. True.

Xavier let out a slow breath. He wasn't trying to be perfect anymore. Not trying to carry it all on his own. He had teammates. Friends. A coach who believed in him. And a pathway forward, drawn in dry-erase marker, waiting to be earned.

He zipped up his hoodie, stepped outside into the soft evening light and jogged to catch up with the others. The tournament was on.

Every detail mattered. Any mistake could end it.

"Charles, wait up," Xavier called as the team started to head off the field.

Charles turned, his boots dragging slightly on the grass. "What's up?"

"You doing alright?" Xavier asked, jogging over. "We've got a break before the next match. How about a kick-around at the park this week? Clear your head. Work on a few moves?"

Charles shrugged, eyes down. "Maybe. Not sure it matters right now."

Xavier placed a hand on his shoulder. "It matters. We're heading into the knockouts, and this team needs your spark back. Don't let one game define you."

For a moment, Charles nodded silently. The rest of Oakridge FC walked ahead, their voices fading into the night air.

As he glanced toward the field one last time, Charles made himself a quiet promise, to find his spark again.

Because the road to the final was only just beginning.

[To be continued in Book 3:
Charles & Jay: Brothers in the Game]

Discover more stories, character bios, and upcoming releases at

www.whitfieldbooks.com.